Death of a Yorkshire Pudding

Albert Smith's Culinary Capers

Recipe 5

Steve Higgs

Pub in Yorkshire with stout and ale aplenty. Red faces sweating with alcohol's influence. Singing fine songs in reverie and ecstasy. Salivating at arrival of that succulent essence.

Tender juicy slices of beef covered with gravy. A splendour when touched by crispy bubbling pudding. Roast potatoes smiling that wicked grin for tongue's activity. Forks and knives clatter in haste for that delight of tasty supping.

Drowning that deliciousness with ale. Rhyming lyrics midst throng of patrons' happiness. Roast beef and Yorkshire pudding you made me hale. I will visit you often and celebrate tummy's warmth in merriness.

Table of Contents:

Chase and Bite

The shout made him spin around on the spot, yanking his human's arm cruelly, which was unfortunate, but Rex recognised a cry of fear when he heard it. His human heard it too but wasn't able to react as swiftly as his canine companion.

It was a bright and glorious day in York where they arrived late yesterday evening on the train from Biggleswade. Neither had ever been to York before, yet it was a beautiful city filled with ancient architecture. There were similar cities in Albert's home county of Kent, but few he could name where the medieval walls of the city were absorbed so completely into the modern look and feel of what came after.

On their way to the station to meet Albert's eldest son, Gary, the shout which distracted them so, came from the other end of a short alleyway running between two buildings. To the left of the alley was a haberdashery, its windows filled with colourful sheets of material artfully arranged. To the right was a franchise bakery selling machine-made pies and sausage rolls. Neither were a factor in the attack occurring less than thirty yards away.

A man in his early sixties, by Albert's reckoning, his briefcase held high to protect his face, was fending off a young man. The victim wore a splendid sky-blue suit complete with waistcoat and pocket watch. On his face were glasses, the frame made from a brushed aluminium that complimented his greying hair. The attacker had startled him but failed in his initial assault for the victim was now facing his assailant and doing his best to protect himself.

The young man had a baton, the kind that comes with a small wrist loop at the handle end so it cannot be dropped or ripped away. His face was covered by a balaclava to make him look like a terrorist - if terrorists wore sportswear, that is.

In the half second between turning to see where the shout came from, and realising there was a mugging in progress, Albert watched the baton swing down from high overhead. It struck the raised briefcase with a whack, the sound echoing in the gap between the buildings.

Rex lunged. Seeing the attack, his natural defensive instincts kicked in. He was trained as a police dog and would be doing the job now were it not for his human handlers' inability to deal with him knowing best all the time. He was held in check by the old man, who held on tight with both hands.

Albert had no way of knowing what might have caused the altercation he was now witness to, but a young man in scruffy sportswear with his face hidden, against one man in a splendid suit equalled robbery in progress in his head and that dictated it was time to intervene. He would have done it himself a few decades ago, but at seventy-eight, giving chase was no longer in his arsenal of possible responses.

Instead, he said, 'Sic 'em, boy,' and opened both his hands.

The leather leash whipped through his open hands as Rex's bunched muscles sprang forward like springs under tension. One moment the dog was stationary, the next he was sprinting down the alleyway.

Rex didn't bother with any nonsense like a warning bark. There was a human to bite and he appeared to have carte blanche permission to get him. This was his kind of challenge and he would not be found lacking. With his head down and his mouth closed, he powered across the street and into the alley. He passed a man who was watching the drama unfold with disbelieving eyes and, more pertinently for Rex, an abandoned slice of pizza. Part-eaten before either being discarded or dropped, it still smelled divine, but chasing and biting was more important than food right now.

The young man with the baton didn't see Albert or hear what he said, but he saw the dog coming. He had his hands on the man's briefcase when he first spotted the dog hurtling his way. At that point, Rex was just entering the alley and still twenty-five yards away. The dog would close the distance in no more than two or three seconds, and sensing that, the attacker abandoned his attempt to get the briefcase.

However, as he let go, so too did the man in the suit. Inevitably, the briefcase fell to the ground, striking the cold stone with one corner and bursting open. To Albert, who was hurrying toward the alley as swiftly as his legs would carry him, it almost looked as if the man in the sky-blue suit had chosen to let it go, perhaps accepting that the contents were not worth injury or worse.

Coming into the alley, Albert passed the same man Rex had, throwing him a quick glance as he silently questioned why it hadn't occurred to him to help the hapless victim twenty yards away. The man was a big unit, broad at the shoulder and with a shaved head that tapered to his trapezius muscles without feeling the need to include a neck.

The man stared open-mouthed at the drama unfolding at the other end of the alley, but when he saw Albert looking his way, guilt at his lack of social responsibility overcame him. He snapped his mouth shut, turned, and walked the other way.

Albert thought about slinging an insult, but there was no time, and his eyes were drawn to the sight ahead. The man in the suit was on the ground now, trying to avoid dirtying his fine clothes while at the same time scrambling to collect all the bundles of money which had spilled from the briefcase onto the stone pavement.

His assailant was running, Rex powering along behind him, and though Albert could see his dog would soon catch the man, he was already at the mouth of the alley and about to vanish from sight. Albert shouted, 'Rex, stop!' even though he doubted his command would achieve much. He wanted the mugging to stop and that was already accomplished. Catching the young man was secondary, and though desirable, the alley opened to a road on the other side where cars were going by every second. If Rex chased the man … well, Albert remembered what happened when Rex chased a man into traffic in Biggleswade and felt no desire for a repeat performance of that event. Worse yet, it could be Rex who got hurt this time.

The young man barrelled into a pedestrian as he came out of the alley. Albert got to see the whole thing, including the part where he grabbed the startled pedestrian, a young woman, and threw her roughly to the pavement to block the dog's path. She cried with shock and threw out her arms to protect herself, screaming something as she pitched forward out of control.

Albert hobbled down the alley as fast as he could muster. Initially, he was chasing Rex and going to the victim's aid. Now there was more than one person in need of help. The man in the business suit, now free of his attacker and the danger he presented, was scooping his money back into the briefcase. No doubt he was reeling from the shock and consequent adrenalin, but he looked to be unharmed which made Albert refocus his attention on Rex and the still-screaming woman.

The young man vanished from Albert's sight, turning left along the pavement. Less than two seconds later, Rex also disappeared, rounding the corner going many times faster than the young man. Rex had to dodge around the woman, who was on her knees now and tearing at her coat to get it open.

'Stop!' barked Rex. 'Or don't stop, it's your choice. But you cannot outrun me, so your only hope to not get bitten on the backside is to lie down and make yourself look defenceless.' Rex loved chasing humans; it had been his favourite part of police dog training. He was aware that at times he could get a little overexcited and rarely bit the exposed padded limb the human target offered him. He knew what he was supposed to do, but where was the fun in that? That was training, and though fun, it was nothing like the real thing when there were proper criminals to chase and catch. They would try to run away, and he would get to run and leap and bite.

Ahead of him, the young man was veering toward the road, heading toward a gap between cars parked along the kerb. Rex could see that his target was going to make it to the gap, but only just because Rex would be on him by then.

With a final bark of, 'Got you!' Rex leapt into the air.

And hit nothing.

The sneaky human had grabbed a lamppost at the very last moment and swung himself around it. The chunk of flesh Rex had been about to sink his teeth into zipped away just as his teeth snapped shut. With a snarl of disbelief, Rex swung his head around, but his body sailed onward through the air to land in the road between two parked cars.

The human had bought himself an extra couple of seconds, nothing more, but as Rex spun himself back around to give chase again, the man swung onto the back of a moped. The moped was already in motion, the driver slowing only to let the passenger get safely on before cranking the throttle again.

In the alleyway, Albert was almost at the man in his flamboyant suit, but did he go to him or to the young woman? The chivalrous part of him directed that he had to attend to the woman first, but then a politically correct voice popped into his head to argue that such views were no longer appropriate, insisting that to favour her suggested he thought the woman less capable of managing. Unable to decide, it was the woman ripping her coat open to reveal the baby tucked inside it that sealed the vote in her favour.

The young mum was screeching with fear and for good reason: the baby was strapped to her front inside a papoose type sling thing and she had fallen on it.

'Goodness are you alright?' he asked, arriving at her side, and doing his best to crouch next to where she knelt.

The baby gurgled up at mummy, clearly unharmed and most likely wondering why mummy had tears streaking down her face.

Sobbing, the young woman managed to start cooing at her child, gently cradling its head which was when Albert noticed the cuts to her hands from breaking her fall. Feeling his eyes flare, he pulled out his phone and began dialling.

'I'm calling an ambulance,' he told her. In the two seconds it took to connect, Albert swung his attention to the man in the suit. 'Sir, are you injured? Did he take anything?' The man's briefcase was clutched to his chest, the contents safely locked back inside, but he wasn't looking at Albert, he was staring down the alleyway, back toward the other street where Rex and Albert had come from. Albert's shout caught his attention, snapping his head around where he gawped, unable to form words.

Doing his best to calm the young mother, Albert was about to repeat his question to the man in the suit when Rex whizzed back past the mouth of the alley from left to right. He was in the road with the traffic and chasing a moped on which the attacker in the balaclava now rode pillion. The sight made Albert's eyes bug out and instantly drew his attention away from either of the victims. Bellowing, 'Rex, no!' had no effect whatsoever. He pushed on his thighs to get to his feet and shouted again as Rex disappeared behind a parked car.

In the road, Rex was incensed that the human opted to cheat. Using a motorised vehicle was not in the rules of chase and bite! The miscreant was getting away, the moped's superior speed enough to outpace Rex, yet he wasn't giving up and the relative difference in speed wasn't that great.

Rex barked his anger as he pounded after the tiny bike. Weighed down by the extra person, it took its sweet time getting up to full speed, but once there it was going to escape if Rex didn't come up with a way to stop it or slow it down.

Rex didn't understand traffic. He got that there were cars and lorries and they went on the road and not the pavement. However, they would be going along a road, all flowing in the same direction and then inexplicably all decide to stop. Then cars would flow in front of them going in a different direction, or perhaps some humans would cross the road. How the decision to all stop was communicated he was yet to fathom, but it was happening now. The line of cars he was running alongside all began to slow as the ones at the front came to a stop. The moped, like Rex, was whipping along the gap between the parked cars and the ones which had been moving. The moped would have to slow down, Rex realised with excitement. They would slow and he would get them then. It would make this game of chase and bite the best ever because the human had cheated and still lost.

However, the moped didn't slow. The passenger was shouting something to the driver - Rex couldn't hear it, there was too much noise, but when they reached the front of the queue of cars and trucks, the moped carried on, whipping across the road which crossed in front of them without slowing down one bit.

Rex heard a cacophony of horns and tyres skidding followed by the sound of two or more cars colliding. The moped sailed through the gap between cars, as drivers in the cross street tried to avoid them by slamming on their brakes.

Unwilling to give up, despite the knowledge that he was running head long into traffic, Rex kept his head down and trusted to luck. The moped slowed to manoeuvre around one car but made it to the other side of the road losing only a few yards. Rex jumped over the bonnet of the same car, gaining yards, but that was as close as he got, for once clear of the junction, the street angled downward enough to give the moped the extra speed it needed to leave Rex behind.

He kept it in sight for as long as he could, but when it made a left turn, Rex was over a hundred yards behind and beginning to slow through fatigue. Out of breath, he slowed to a steady jog and followed his nose.

Back at the scene of the attack, Albert was trying to bury his concern over Rex. He hadn't been able to watch as the moped and dog flew through the junction against the traffic, but despite hiding his face, he saw Rex make it to the other side and then vanish from sight as the street angled down. There was nothing he could do except hope Rex would stop running before he left the city. Shortly, Albert would excuse himself and go looking for him, rather than risk Rex coming back and trying to negotiate the road for a second time.

Before he could do that, he needed to manage the situation around him. Rosie, as he'd quickly discovered the young mother's name to be, had protected the baby at the expense of her own hands and knees, all of which were torn, but the baby was unharmed, mercifully. The man had assured Albert that he was going to be okay, though he was white as a sheet, and insisted he could wait while Albert tended to the young lady and infant. With an ambulance on route and the police alerted, Albert helped Rosie back toward a car parked at the edge of the road. There, he convinced her to take the weight off her feet by leaning on it.

'If you feel faint at all, just put your head down and call for me,' he urged her. 'I'm going to check on the gentleman who was attacked.'

Rosie murmured, 'Okay,' but her attention was all on the baby which was beginning to get uppity.

'Hello,' Albert said as he approached the man in the suit. 'How are you feeling now?' The colour was coming back to the man's cheeks and he didn't seem to be injured. 'Can I ask your name? Mine's Albert,' Albert said to get the man talking.

The man was using his left hand to brush a mark from his suit where he knelt it on the pavement earlier to retrieve his money. He looked across at Albert when he spoke. 'Alan Crystal.' He switched his briefcase from right hand to left, extending his right hand to shake. 'Was that your dog?' he asked.

The question caused Albert to wince with worry and check back along the road to see if Rex was anywhere in sight. 'Yes,' he answered. 'I'm beginning to worry about him.'

'He did me quite the favour then,' the man admitted. Picking up his briefcase once more, he joined Albert in looking down the street. 'No sign of him?'

Other people were joining them now. Albert didn't think anyone other than he and Rex had seen the attack, but it was clear to anyone looking now, that something had happened, and Rosie's distressed state was plain to see. He wanted to ask Alan about the surprising amount of money in his briefcase. In his experience, no one in their right mind carried around bundles of notes like that. It was the sort of thing a person saw in a movie where a ransom was being paid. The uninvited thought made him scratch his chin as another question surfaced. He couldn't ask any of them though, not just because it was none of his business, but because the small gathering of concerned people was growing more numbers by the second.

The baby was really starting to wind up, the sound coming from it roughly the same volume as an air raid siren. 'Can one of you help me?' Rosie asked, her tone pleading and still coming out as a sob.

Both men sprung to her aid. 'What can we do, my dear?' asked Albert.

'I need to get the baby out of the sling, but my hands are really sore.' Albert willingly approached, but once standing in front of her, he was struck by how complex the simple task might be.

Staring at the baby, and definitely not the woman's voluminous chest, he cautiously lifted his hands, but paused more than a foot away as he twisted his hands this way and that. 'How do I ...'

Rosie came to him, bumping herself away from the car, 'You just have to pull the folds apart a little and reach your hands down inside. Grab Teddy under his arms and pull him upwards. He'll just slide out.

The small, but gathering, crowd around them spewed forth a volunteer. 'Here, I'll do it,' said a youth of about fourteen with a leering look. His mates laughed as he stepped forward with his hands already in the famous grab-your-boobs pose.

Rosie frowned and was probably about to say something cutting when Albert distracted her by tackling the task. The wailing noise from little Teddy defied belief, yet there seemed no end to it. Rosie had her head turned to one side since Albert was right inside her personal space, close enough that he caught a trace of her perfume when he slid his hands in around the baby.

Sirens boomed into life a street over, the sound echoing off the buildings. To Albert it was a welcome noise that meant the cavalry would soon arrive to rescue him. Focused on getting the task done so he could hand the baby to someone else and protect his hearing before Teddy made him deaf, Albert probably should have questioned why the baby was so squishy. A heartbeat later, as he tried to lift him and realisation dawned, his head shot around to look into Rosie's face.

'That is not the baby you have hold of,' she growled.

Quickly opening his right hand and groping, quite literally, around, he managed to find something that felt much more like a tiny ribcage. With a final scream of success from Teddy, Albert pulled the baby clear and Rosie, injured hands still held aloft, was able to step away.

When finally, the police arrived ten seconds later, Teddy was back with his mother and beginning to settle. The moment the police got within earshot, he started toward them, it was time to find Rex.

Lost Dog

Rex followed the moped to where it had turned off the road and then carried on for a distance trying to track the scent. He hadn't been able to get a decent enough sample of the man's scent as he chased him. There were too many other smells around to be sure which was distinctly his. In contrast, the smell left behind by the moped was easy to follow. At least it was initially, but it was dissipating on the air so that by the time he made the turn down which they had vanished, it too was gone.

He snuffled around, looking for anything that might give him a clue as to where they might have gone, but found nothing and, disappointed, accepted defeat. Humans were not supposed to win the game of chase and bite. They never had before, so as he trudged back the way he had come, he promised himself that if he ever got another chance at the same human, he wouldn't fail again.

Hold on though: where am I? The thought surprised Rex as if it snuck up and jumped out on him. He was in a strange city, on a strange street and even following his nose wouldn't work because all the smells were unfamiliar.

Perplexed, he sat for a moment, lifting his nose to the sky to sample the air. His human was around here somewhere, he hadn't gone that far chasing the moped, surely.

Back at the scene of the attack, Albert was beginning to become annoyed. 'You say you lost your dog?' the police officer attempted to confirm.

'He chased the attacker. I already explained this. I *am* going to look for him.' Albert had attempted to leave Rosie and Alan the moment the police arrived. He would return once he had Rex, but an officer blocked his path, insisting they needed to speak with him before he went anywhere. The officer, a man in his early thirties with a trim beard and watery eyes, did not look ready to let Albert go anywhere. Seeing that he was about to argue again, Albert leaned into his face. 'Arrest me if you wish. Otherwise get out of my way. I'm going to find my dog.'

'For goodness sake, go with him, Yates,' snapped the other officer, a woman who had to be most of a decade younger than her partner. She was of Asian descent, middle eastern, Albert believed, and unwilling to discuss the subject. Before Yates could argue, she followed up her comment. 'He wants to find his dog. Help him and then we can ask questions.' She nodded her head toward the road where another police car had just stopped, its roof lights flashing as the two men inside got out. 'I've got all the help I need.'

Biting down an angry retort for his younger colleague, Yates levelled his eyes at Albert. 'Which way did you say the dog went, sir?'

Albert didn't particularly want the help, but he wasn't going to argue either. He nodded his head down the street. 'This way.' There was no need for conversation and neither man spoke until they reached the junction almost a hundred yards ahead. There, yet more cops were arriving to deal with the multiple accidents the moped caused, and Albert could hear the chatter on PC Yates's radio as they tried to sort out the mess and get traffic flowing again.

Traffic was at a standstill in every direction, making it easy to cross the road. Rex would have been able to safely return, but there was no sign of the dog.

'You said it is a large German Shepherd?' Yates tried to confirm even though Albert had been unambiguous in his description.

Albert stared down the road, frowning with worry, and didn't bother to answer the police officer who clearly wasn't interested in helping to look for Rex. With hands cupped around his mouth, Albert called for his dog and made whistling noises.

'Do you know which way he went, sir?' Yates asked.

Albert's frown deepened when Rex failed to appear and he didn't turn his head when he answered, 'This way. He chased the moped with the assailants clear across the junction. I lost sight of him as he dipped below the horizon.'

Yates leaned his head toward his radio, pressing the send switch before telling anyone who might be listening about the missing dog. Albert wasn't happy about abandoning the search, not that he could really call it a search when all they had done was walk to the junction and look down one street, but Rex could be anywhere.

By the time they got back to Rosie and Alan's location, an ambulance with paramedics had arrived. Alan was giving a statement to a sergeant but making it clear that he needed to move on and couldn't tell them much. 'He tried to hit me with the baton,' Albert heard him say. 'His face was covered by a balaclava and he wore gloves. What I could see of him was Caucasian, I think, but the only bit of skin visible was round his eyes, so he might have been mixed race, or Mediterranean. I would judge his age to be late teens or early twenties, but I must admit I am basing that on his shape and clothing.'

Albert acknowledged that the description was accurate. However, Alan was avoiding mention of the money in his briefcase. The attacker must have known about it – he went straight for it. Alan gave a decent description of the attacker's clothing, even getting the designer labels right which surprised Albert – few people were ever that observant, especially in the heat of the moment.

They asked Albert what he saw, which allowed Albert to corroborate the same details. He knew it gave the police almost nothing to go on: if the assailant had the slightest trace of sense, he would ditch the clothing and burn it. No one managed to record the number plate on the moped, or even got a good enough look at it to determine make and model.

'He was after the man's briefcase,' Albert said. 'I saw him grab it. My dog interrupted the theft, or he would have made off with it, I'm sure.'

PC Yates noted his comment, but in a big city it was a small crime and there were no significant injuries, and nothing had been taken. Any follow up would be half-hearted as it got lost beneath more pressing cases.

Taking himself off to one side for a moment, Albert took his phone from his jacket pocket and called his son. Gary was on the express train from London, which travelled from London to York in two hours and was due to arrive any moment. Albert had been heading to the station when the attack occurred and was supposed to be waiting for his son in a coffee shop inside the station. Thinking it best to let him know, he started talking the moment the call was answered.

'Gary, it's dad. I've got caught up and will be a few minutes adrift getting to the station. Sorry. Can you find a coffee shop, or a pub and I'll meet you there shortly?'

To Albert's surprise, Gary said, 'No, Dad. There are leaves on the line.'

'Leaves on the line,' Albert repeated. 'How late will you be?' That a few leaves falling in autumn could disrupt travel beggared belief in Albert's opinion and secretly, he suspected the rail companies used it as a catch-all excuse at this time of year because no one could argue with it.

'Only about half an hour,' grumbled Gary. 'It's okay. I have a book I'm reading. I'll let you know when I get there.' Albert was waiting for his son to ask what could possibly have caused his own delay in arriving at the station. He didn't want to explain that he was involved in another incident, and he certainly didn't want to tell him he couldn't find Rex. Thankfully, Gary said, 'We've just gone into a tunn …' and the line when dead.

Pocketing his phone once more, Albert went to check on Rosie. Mum was in the back of the ambulance where her hands were being cleaned and dressed. Two of the fingers on her right hand had been taped together. Her son, Teddy, was being cradled by another paramedic, a man in his forties with a bald head and big smile. He was pulling faces at the infant, trying to keep the little one's mood even while his mother was attended to.

Albert wanted to ask if she was all right, but she got in first. 'I forgot to thank you for helping me back there,' Rosie said, peering around the side of the paramedic to look at Albert. 'Did you find your dog?'

'Not yet,' said Albert, trying to squash down the ball of worry forming in his gut. 'I'm sure he's fine. The police will pick him up begging at a restaurant I expect.' The joke was for his benefit, not anyone else's and he managed a tight smile. 'Are you okay?' he asked.

She shook her head and a small tear escaped her right eye. 'I'm fine,' she lied. 'I have to get to work.'

'With your hands like that?' he questioned. 'Surely, you can be granted a day off.'

She shook her head again, more vigorously this time, and refused to make eye contact. 'It's a temporary contract. If I don't turn up, I don't get paid.'

17

Albert felt an upwelling of empathy for the young mother. From her clothing and tatty shoes, he could see she wasn't well off. It caused a natural desire to help her though he couldn't work out how he might achieve that.

The paramedic finished what he was doing and stood up, hunched over a little in the back of the ambulance. 'That's about the best I can do here. Your fingers are most likely just bruised from being hyperextended. They will hurt for a few weeks but there is no sign that anything is broken and very little a doctor can do other than prescribe pain medication.'

'Which you said I can get over the counter or from my own GP,' Rosie added. The paramedic agreed and joined his colleague entertaining Teddy. Rosie held up her hand to study it, wincing when she tried to flex her fingers. 'This is going to be a problem,' she muttered.

There was nothing left for Albert to say: Rosie was treated, and though her hand most likely hurt, there wasn't a thing Albert could do about that. He was about to wish her luck when Yates tapped him on the shoulder.

'I think we found your dog, sir.'

Rex waited for a while. He couldn't measure it in minutes; he had no concept of time other than to observe that it was time to eat, or time to go for a walk. The sun came up and that was the start of the day. Later, the sun would set again. However, after determining that his human wasn't coming for him, he started walking. Any direction was as good as another, so he set off. As luck would have it, he was going in completely the wrong direction to the one which would lead him back to his human. Without a scent to follow, he couldn't tell.

After a few minutes, he chanced upon a man in uniform. He recognised uniforms as a positive thing since everyone he met as a puppy was wearing one. He had been a police dog and though this man was wearing a different uniform, it still also looked quite similar. Plus, the man smelled like food.

Coming nearer, Rex could see more uniforms. They were climbing onto a large red vehicle which was inside a large building with tall roller doors. The door in front of the big red vehicle had just finished ascending. The man he saw first hadn't noticed him yet, but he did when Rex decided going inside was a good idea.

Trotting past his legs, the man turned to see the giant German Shepherd letting himself into the fire station. 'Hey, dog!' he called, but Rex was already inside and looking about.

Inside the fire station, and jogging to get to the fire truck, Station Officer Hamilton spotted the dog coming in and altered his course to intercept it. At forty-seven, Edward Hamilton had most likely advanced as far up the ladder as he was going to get, but he was happy running a station of his own and treated his firefighters like family. He had a dog of his own, a beagle, at home and considered himself to be a dog person.

'Hey, boy,' he called, getting the dog's attention with his friendly tone.

Rex trotted toward the man who was now down on one knee and showing his empty hands.

'You found a stray, boss?' asked one of his firefighters, hanging out of the truck when the engine coughed and sprung to life.

Raising his voice to be heard, he said, 'This is no stray. Look at his coat. He's beautiful. Well fed too.' Feeling his neck fur, he found the collar hidden within it and read the tag. 'Rex.'

Rex turned his head, giving the human a lick on his chin in greeting.

From above them all, a window on the first floor opened and another firefighter leaned out. 'Hey, boss. There's a call from dispatch about a loose German Shepherd in the area. It's something to do with the accident they want us to sort out.'

Station Officer Hamilton looked back down at the dog. 'I guess that's you then, fella. We'd better get going though. We have to cut someone from their car.'

The fire fighters had just been called to an accident less than half a mile away from their station where the police needed their specialist equipment and rescue techniques to deal with a man trapped inside his mangled car. The likelihood that they had the lost dog in their possession was high enough for them to lift him into the truck and take him along.

Their guess proved right as the dog started jumping and bouncing around on the end of his lead the moment they opened the door to the fire truck. His human was here; Rex could smell him!

Albert spotted him easily; it was hard to miss the firefighters trying in vain to calm the overexcited giant dog in the cab of a fire truck.

'I guess Rex belongs to you,' said Station Officer Hamilton with a laugh, leaving the truck behind to meet the dog's owner.

Albert managed to combine a chuckle and a sigh. 'Has he been any bother?'

His question drew another laugh from the station officer. 'We did nearly crash twice because Rex wanted to see where we were going, but once we got his collar attached to a lashing point it was okay.'

Rex arrived dragging a burly firefighter behind him as, with single-minded determination, he made his way back to his human. Albert clicked the fingers of his right hand as he moved it upwards through the air. Rex obediently jumped onto his back legs and placed his front paws on Albert's shoulders. Albert had to brace himself against the weight, but he found this was easier than crouching or bending.

He ruffled Rex's fur and gave the dog a hug. The station officer was already backing away. 'If you'll excuse me, I am needed elsewhere.' He turned and jogged away before Albert got a chance to thank him, and when he returned to the ambulance to check on Rosie once more, the sad young mother in her tatty shoes was already gone.

The crowd of onlookers had gotten bored and drifted away, and even the police were packing up. Alan Crystal had given his statement and gone on his way without Albert seeing him go or getting the chance to ask him about the large amount of money and his desire to omit telling the police about it.

It felt like a mystery to solve, but Albert was an old man in an old and unfamiliar city. He was here for the weekend because there was a big Yorkshire pudding baking competition, not to involve himself in solving what might have been a random mugging. Pushing thoughts of the last hour from his mind, Albert set off for the station again. It was time for a cup of tea.

Waiting

Sitting at a table for two in a café opposite York train station, Albert was troubled by the plate before him. More accurately, it was what sat on the plate that troubled him, even though it had been his selection.

Albert thought of himself as a man of simple tastes; he ate the same dishes repeatedly and had done his entire life, rarely stretching his tastebuds or challenging himself with something new.

He succumbed to peer pressure in the eighties and tasted a curry one night. He enjoyed it, he somewhat begrudgingly admitted, and had visited Indian restaurants since, he only ever ate the one dish though: a chicken Madras.

So the café menu boasting sweet Yorkshire puddings, was almost too much for his poor brain to handle. On his plate was a chocolate profiterole but one made not with choux pastry, but with a Yorkshire pudding batter. Yorkshire puddings were a savoury dish and, so far as Albert was concerned, that ended the conversation. Yet faced with a new challenge, he chose to remind himself that he was on a culinary tour of the British Isles and selected the sweet treat even though he felt deeply suspicious about it.

He got one for Rex Harrison too – a bacon and egg one in his case. Rex harboured no such suspicions and ate it in one bite. Sitting next to his human, Rex's head rose a foot above the table, placing his mouth in line with the cake thing on his human's plate. His human did not seem inclined to eat it, which Rex was only too happy with – he would take one for the team, so to speak, and save the old man from it.

Albert silently scolded himself for being so cowardly, picked the cake/pudding up and bit into it. A blob of freshly whipped cream went up his nose, but otherwise the profiterole was a delight and little different from eating one made with choux pastry. There remained, to Albert's simplistic way of thinking, something fundamentally wrong about the dish, but he could not in good conscience say anything negative about it.

His phone rang, the screen facing uppermost on the table where he placed it displaying the name of the caller. Unfortunately, Albert couldn't read it because he didn't have his reading glasses on. Even holding it at arm's length and squinting, the caller's name refused to swim into focus. With a sigh, he accepted defeat and thumbed the green answer button.

'Albert Smith.'

'Dad, it's Gary. The train is just pulling into the station. I'll be on the platform in about a minute. Are you nearby?'

Two minutes later, Albert spotted his first-born son making his way along the platform. Gary wasn't tall, not by twenty-first century standards, but he wasn't short either at six feet two inches and that made him easy to pick out from the press of people making their way through the turnstyle at the end of the platform. Always happy to see the man who had once, long ago, been the tiny boy who filled his heart with joy, Albert couldn't, and saw no reason to, stop the broad smile spreading across his face.

'Hi, Dad,' Gary shook his father's hand. He had a backpack over his left shoulder with all the things he felt he would need for a two-night stay in York.

Gripping his son's hand tightly, Albert replied, 'Hello, son. Thank you for coming.' Albert's suitcase and backpack were already at the bed and breakfast his daughter Selina had booked for them many weeks ago. Originally, it was only booked for Albert and Rex, but Gary was added at his insistence just a week ago. Albert's three children were taking it in turns to babysit him through the misguided belief that he might get into

24

trouble without them. He could have felt insulted, but in truth, he chose to embrace the imposition because it meant he got to spend time with his children.

He felt especially glad to have Gary along because he had a subject to discuss with him. He'd already sent him a message about it when he was on the train from Biggleswade last night.

Setting off, back toward the exit from the station, Gary fell into step beside his father. 'Are we still off to the Yorkshire pudding competition tomorrow?' he asked. Gary wanted to avoid the daft subject his father was undoubtedly going to raise sooner or later. The message he got last night made him question if his father really was going senile now. The old man had asked about any cases of chefs or restauranteurs going missing, or of food being stolen in bulk. Not just ordinary food though, speciality foods. His father was harbouring some crazy idea about a master criminal like he was living in a James Bond movie or something.

Albert fielded his son's question. 'We certainly are, Gary. There's all manner of attraction to tempt us. There's an attempt at the world's largest Yorkshire pudding and I read that this year's best Yorkshire pudding champion will win a big cash prize and get a shot at having their recipe taken on by Bentley Brothers supermarket chain.' He fell silent for a moment, then remembered to say, 'Would you believe I ate a Yorkshire pudding filled with cream and covered with chocolate sauce just before you arrived?'

Gary pulled a face of disgust. 'That sounds horrible,' he managed around a grimace.

Albert chuckled at his son's expression. 'I know what you are saying, but it was really quite nice. They used the pudding instead of choux pastry.'

'Why?'

Gary's question only got a shrug in response.

The two men and Rex the dog were walking along Queen Street close to the city wall trail. It was a cool, but pleasant day and little conversation was required as they meandered through York taking in the sights. They turned left along Nunnery Lane, keeping the ancient city wall to their left. At a sign erected to inform visitors and tourists about the wall, they paused to read, discovering the fortifications were mostly built by the Romans more than a thousand years ago.

'That's workmanship for you,' commented Gary. 'Modern builders wouldn't build a wall that would last a thousand years.'

Albert pursed his lips, considering his son's statement. 'I'm sure you are right, Gary. However, builders now are not considering invading hordes as they draw up their plans.'

Gary conceded the point and they moved on. After a minute or so of walking, Gary spotted a sign to the Yorkshire Pudding Museum. 'Is that where we are heading?' he asked with a head nod at the brown tourist sign.

'Indeed. Your sister booked us a B&B a couple of streets over from it. We can drop your bag there first if you like.'

They followed the sign, which led them through Victoria Bar Gate, one of the original gateways into the city. Albert marvelled that a thousand years ago, guards of some kind must have stood on the exact same flag stones his feet were now passing over. What stories the ancient wall could tell.

Their bed and breakfast was a pleasant enough place. It was owned and run by a couple in their sixties. Boasting just three rooms, Albert and Gary had two of them at the rear of the house. Mrs Morton greeted Albert and Rex at the door, looking around Albert at the man standing behind him.

'This must be your son,' she guessed, knowing he would be arriving today after a chat with Albert over breakfast.

With his bag dropped and most of the afternoon to fill, the trio set off again. Albert was yet to raise the subject of the master criminal and had been waiting to see if Gary would do so first. It had been most of an hour since they met at the station which Albert decided was enough.

They were approaching the museum and could see a bright banner erected on the front façade. It bragged *Fifty-Seventh Annual World Yorkshire Pudding Championships* in bold letters three feet high. As they turned off the street toward the main entrance Albert paused, his feet stopping of their own accord as he stared down the street.

Gary's feet hadn't stopped, carrying him six feet before he noticed his father was no longer at his side. Wearing a bemused smile, he retraced his steps. 'Everything all right, Dad? Your feet still work?'

Albert scrunched his face. 'I just saw someone.'

Gary's worry that his father might be getting a little senile spiked again because there was no one in sight anywhere. Electing to play along, Gary said, 'Are they gone now?' However, having said the words, he worried what he might then do if his father claimed he could still see them.

Frowning deeply, Albert looked at his son. 'Can you see them?' he demanded to know. 'Of course they're gone. There was a man in the alleyway when the mugging occurred. I thought I just saw him again – the same black leather jacket and lack of neck.' Albert was convinced it was the same man, which he might have chalked up to coincidence were it not for the man spotting Albert and ducking down a side road.

Sensing that his son was waiting impatiently, and no desire to listen to his father's wild theories, Albert gritted his teeth and dismissed the notion that the man had just deliberately avoided him. Staring toward the museum again, he asked, 'Did you get a chance to look into my question about missing persons before you left?'

Gary kept the sigh he felt inside. It wasn't so much that he despaired of his father, it was much more the case that he loved him, and having lost mum just a little more than a year ago, he didn't want to face the possibility that dad was going a little loopy. 'I didn't, dad, if I am being honest. In fact, to be brutally honest, I chose not to.'

Albert let his eyebrows rise and pulled them back under control as he said, 'I see.' He wanted to be annoyed; an emotion distinctly south of angry, which he never wanted to feel towards his children, but he was disappointed and shared that with his son. 'I suppose you believe there is nothing to investigate.'

This time Gary did sigh. They had ground to a halt to have their discussion outside, rather than take it into the ticket booth they could see just inside the door.

Rex parked his bottom on the path. The humans were talking about something. It didn't interest him. What did was the familiar scent coming out of the doors of the building they were stopped outside. It was the man he had rescued earlier, the one who was getting attacked. Rex lifted his nose to sample the air again: he was certain.

Coincidence was not a concept Rex understood. Things happened or they didn't. If you could smell it, then it was true. The man in the sky-blue suit was here, but then he had to be somewhere. Above his ears, his human and his human's pup – Rex understood the pack relationship – were beginning to get agitated.

'I never said there was a master criminal at work!' snapped Albert, feeling affronted that Gary was suggesting he needed to look for his marbles because they were lost.

Gary held up his hands defensively. 'That's what it sounded like, Dad. You asked me to look for missing person cases where the missing person was a chef of some kind, or linked to the food, catering, or restaurant industries. When I asked why, you said that someone might be trying to forcibly recruit them.'

Albert opened his mouth to argue again but, recalling the messages back and forth the previous evening, he had to admit those were more or less his exact words. He was about to come at the discussion from a different angle when Rex suddenly got to his feet and lurched forward, tugging his arm.

Turning his head to see what might have attracted the dog's attention, he found the man in the flamboyant suit coming his way.

'Hello,' beamed Alan Crystal, leaving the museum to greet the men outside. Approaching with his right hand outstretched, he gushed, 'I'm so pleased to see you again so soon. In all the excitement earlier, I completely forgot to thank you for coming to my rescue.'

'You rescued him?' asked Gary in a whisper from the side of his mouth.

Albert shook Alan's hand. 'That's quite alright. I found my dog,' he pointed out.

'So you did,' nodded Alan, taking in the dog sniffing his suit. 'He's quite the specimen.' Bending down to speak with Rex, he said, 'Thank you for chasing that man away.'

Rex accepted the thanks graciously, wondering if perhaps there ought to be a gravy bone involved somewhere, and still feeling irked that he hadn't caught his target.

Switching focus from Rex to Gary, Alan thrust his hand toward the younger man who had to be the old man's son given the marked similarity in features. 'Pleased to meet you. I'm Alan Crystal, the curator of this fine museum. Your father did me quite the favour earlier.' He stopped pumping Gary's hand to ruffle Rex's ears again. 'This one too, of course.'

Now that he had his hand back, Gary folded his arms and looked down at his father. 'Okay, Dad, what did I miss?'

'It was nothing really,' Albert began to protest, but Alan was having none of it.

'Nonsense, dear fellow.' He glanced behind to the museum entrance. 'You were coming to the museum? Let me arrange special VIP passes. It's the least I can do. There's a big event here tomorrow,' he started to tell them as he back pedalled toward the entrance, then laughed at himself. 'I'm sure you didn't miss the sign. Will you still be here tomorrow? I can tell by your accents that you are not local.'

'Visiting tomorrow was to be the primary purpose of our visit to York,' Albert explained. 'I've come here to learn how to make a Yorkshire pudding.' To Albert, it seemed embarrassing to tell people he couldn't manage so simple a task at his age, especially standing in the entrance to a museum dedicated to the famous dish. Yet it was with glee that the museum curator received the news.

Clapping his hands together, he cheered, 'Well this is wonderful. I shall arrange a private lesson for you both.' He spun around to face the direction of travel and led them both into the old building. 'Come now, gentlemen. I have so much to share with you. I am also the event organiser and chief judge, you see.'

After a brief exchange with the man inside the ticket booth, who Albert at first thought to be a mannequin because he looked so lifeless, Albert and Gary were handed two passes on lanyards. They were for the competition tomorrow and had the following day's date on them. However, Alan assured them there was no need to buy a ticket for today's entry to the museum itself. He led them on a short walking tour of the museum, which wasn't a big place and set only on one floor of what they learned to be the former house of a famous eighteenth century poet laureate. Neither Albert nor Gary had ever heard of the writer in question but chose not to voice their ignorance since the curator was talking about the person's work and achievements in excited tones.

Rex caught a trace of cat on the air and wrinkled his nose with displeasure. There were very few things worse than squirrels in his opinion, but cats were at the top of the list. They had such terrible attitudes and back home he knew there were some that came into his garden at night just to do their business because he kept them out during the day. Were they bothering to defile his human's flowers beds while Rex was away? Or did they see no point because he wasn't there to be angered by their insult?

'Through here is the entrance to the marquee,' Alan announced, leading the party through a door at the rear of the museum.

Albert stopped by a wall where something was clearly missing. It wasn't the first space where sun and time had faded the paint on the wall to leave a shadow where a missing something ought to be. 'Do you have items in for cleaning?' he asked, curious.

Alan's expression turned serious. 'No. We've had some thefts. Unbelievable, isn't it? It's not just historic pictures and artefacts though, the thieves broke into my office and made off with a computer and an office printer we had on hire. The police were not much help, sad to say.'

Albert could understand that – some stolen goods were just impossible to track down, but what value could an artefact from a Yorkshire pudding museum have?

'Are the thefts recent?' Gary asked, a pertinent question from a serving police officer.

Alan nodded. 'Unfortunately, yes. They spread over the last few months. Inexplicably, there is no sign of break in. The police were not able to determine how the thieves might be able to get in and out.' Keen to change the subject, Alan led them away from the missing museum pieces. 'In previous years, visitors have been guided around the building to get to the competition and championships, but this year I felt it was time for a change. Everyone will come through the museum and be treated to the wonders inside. It will really spread the word about our county's most famous dish.'

'And ruin the carpets,' snapped a voice from behind them.

All three men spun around to look where the voice had come from and Rex growled for lazing in the man's arms was an overweight Burmese cat. Its tail dangled over the man's left arm, twitching in a way that made Rex want to bite it.

'Oh, a dog,' said the cat. 'That's what the terrible smell is.'

Rex growled some more, giving fair warning of retribution to come if the cat didn't learn some manners.

Alan found himself the wrong side of his guests and had to go around them to approach the man. 'Now then, Brian, we discussed this at length already and the committee agreed I was right.' He was being diplomatic in his response, Albert thought, but it had little impact on the man whose eyes would cut through steel if he glared any harder. Alan saw fit to introduce the unpleasant man. 'Gentlemen, this is Brian Pumphrey, the deputy head of the event committee.'

Brian was a tiny, squat man, less than five feet tall. Unkindly, Albert remarked in his head that with the addition of a beard and fishing rod, he could model as a garden ornament. Like Alan, he wore a suit, yet his was a sombre brown and green tweed.

'I am the rightful event organiser who was unfairly ousted by political shenanigans,' snapped Brian, glaring even harder at the museum curator.

With a sigh, Alan said, 'Brian, we have been through this. The mayor believed my concept for the future of the event was vastly superior to yours.'

'He never got to hear mine though, did he, Alan?' Brian said in a candy-laced voice. It was clearly an old argument that refused to die. Speaking again before Alan could find a retort, he demanded, 'Who are these men? Are they here to fix the portable heating? It's about time you got here. Hop to it now. I want that working within the hour.'

Albert's eyebrows took a hike to the top of his forehead, but he didn't need to answer him because Alan was doing so.

'Brian, these men are my personal guests, and you are not in charge this year,' he insisted with forced politeness.

'More's the pity,' he snapped without bothering to look Alan's way. 'Look at what has become of our beloved championships. It's a shambles, Alan. The competition has become a spectacle and this awful world record attempt, well it's just ... it's gawdy. That's what it is.' Then a sly grin

34

stole across Brian's face. 'I shall enjoy it immensely when they fail though. What will the mayor think of that, Alan?'

Showing remarkable control, Alan asked, 'What are you doing here anyway, Brian. There is nothing that needs your attention today.'

'I came to see how badly the preparations for my precious championships were proceeding. I'm sorry to say things are far worse than I imagined they could be.'

'Perhaps we should just go and come back tomorrow,' suggested Gary, hoping he and his dad might slip away for a couple of pints and avoid the argument which appeared to be nearing eruption point.

Alan swung his head back around to pierce both men with a politician's smile. 'Nonsense, dear fellow. I plan to show you all the sights. Brian was just leaving after all. Weren't you, Brian?' His tone made sure the question sounded like an order, but it bounced off Brian like grease on Teflon.

'Leaving? I think not. There's far too much to be done. People are counting on me, even if the mayor was foolish enough to let you ruin things this year.' Alan undoubtedly had a response on the tip of his tongue, but Brian was no longer listening. He was walking away, the cat's head poking around the nape of his left elbow to give Rex a look of disgust. 'And get that dog out of here,' Brian commented as he walked away.

'Visitors are encouraged to bring pets!' Alan shouted at Brian's back, his anger finally making it to the surface.

'Not ones that big,' Brian shouted over his shoulder without looking. 'He's smelly too. Fluffikins didn't like him and that's good enough for me.'

35

Brian vanished back inside the museum, disappearing from sight around a corner and shutting off any further chance to retort.

Gary and Albert were silent for a moment while their host gathered himself. 'Goodness, that man is unpleasant,' he told them after taking, holding, and exhaling a deep breath. 'You know, I would not be surprised if he were here only to sabotage my efforts.' Albert gave him a single raised eyebrow; he wasn't sure what other response might be appropriate. He didn't like Brian, but that was based only on Brian's vocal opinion of Rex.

Rex nudged his human's leg. 'If they come back, can I eat the cat?'

Albert started down at Rex. The dog was trying to convey something, Albert was sure of it. 'Something to do with the cat?' he guessed.

Rex bounded up onto all four paws and wagged his tail. 'Yes! Yes, that's right, the cat. It has a terrible attitude and I should be allowed to teach it some manners. I'll just bite off an inch or two of its tail. How about that?'

Albert scrunched up his face in concentration as he attempted in vain to decipher what the dog might be trying to tell him. 'The cat offered you some kind of insult and now you wish to claim retribution.'

Rex twirled on the spot. 'Oh, my goodness! You actually got it! Yes, let's go get that cat!'

Alan clapped his hands together. 'How about we put that unpleasant episode behind us, and I show you the preparations for tomorrow's attempt to break the world record for the largest Yorkshire pudding? The chap from Guinness arrives in the morning.' Alan was already striding away through the large marquee.

36

The marquee was light and airy, as they always are. It was also massive, stretching thirty metres across and at least a hundred metres in the other direction. Then they discovered there were yet more parts of it they could not see as there were equivalent sized marquees extending from each side at the far end where viewed from the air it would look like a giant tee. At the apex of the tee was a raised platform, which could be better described as a stage, Albert decided. It was devoid of any clutter or furniture, but a team of sound engineers were running cables and testing the public address system.

A large woman with unkempt hair and a ruddy complexion spotted Alan and rushed over to him. She held a clipboard in her left hand and pencil in her right. Overall, her appearance was that of someone with too many things to do and too little help.

'Ah, Mr Crystal, I thought you would like to know that Mr Pumphrey has been in here *helping out* again.' The way she said it removed any ambiguity over whether she thought his help was helpful or not.

'I'll have another word with him, Sarah, thank you. How are things going overwise?' Alan asked.

She blew out a breath of exasperation. 'Well, the gas engineers finally got the system operational, so that's a big relief. They said something about being unable to equalise the pressure under the giant pan. Anyway, it's working now, you'll be pleased to hear. The sound engineers are almost finished, but we do have two no-shows on the stall holders. Maisy is trying to contact them now to see if they are still coming because we have plenty of others we turned down who can fill their spots.'

Alan exchanged a few words with Sarah, and she bustled away again, shouting at someone who wasn't doing what he ought to be doing in her opinion.

37

'I couldn't manage without her,' he commented as they moved away. 'Unlike Brian, who I don't need at all, but cannot get rid of.'

Gary asked, 'Why not?'

Alan sucked air in through his teeth. 'He's part of the furniture. He's been head of the event committee for years, and until he does something that would justify removing him, I can see no way of freeing myself. Besides, he will be back running the event next year. I just wanted to show the city what this competition could be with a little bit of imagination and effort. This is to be our largest event ever,' Alan boasted as he led them through the various stalls. Some were those of professional traders, there to sell their wares and getting set up in advance. Others were from local charity groups; another subject Alan spoke of rapidly and frequently. They were to be located in the first part of the marquee through which everyone would funnel on their way in due to Alan's decision to bring them in through the museum.

Reaching the far end where the marquee stretched to the left and right, yet another voice rang out with an angry undertone. 'Mr Crystal! I want a word wi' thee!'

Angry Competitors

Wondering what fresh hell this might be and beginning to regret accepting the VIP treatment from the event organiser, Albert slowly swivelled himself around to see a man in baker's whites approaching. He was in his fifties, with a jowly jaw line which gave his face the look of a bulldog.

Alan greeted him with a smile. 'Mr Ross, is the preparation area to your liking? Have you found everything you need?'

'Nevermind all that, Mr Crystal,' Mr Ross wasn't to have his intentions diverted. 'I'm a fair man and I speaks my mind.' Alan's smile remained in place as he attempted to encourage Mr Ross to speak his mind. He didn't get the chance to because Mr Ross just kept on talking. 'There's something afoot here, Mr Crystal. Some teams seem to have preferential positioning in the competition hall.'

'Yeah,' said a second man, now arriving behind Mr Ross. A woman was with him, his wife probably, Albert decided. 'That bunch from Wetherby are acting as if they don't need to do any test baking. They've been asking us why we are bothering and trying to goad me into placing a side bet on the outside. They seem to know which heat they are in, but the draw hasn't taken place yet.'

'Aye,' echoed Mr Ross. 'There's summit' not right 'ere, I tell thee.'

Alan's face coloured slightly as he tried to defend himself. 'I can assure you both, there is nothing amiss with the arrangements. The preparation area was made available today for the various teams to familiarise themselves with layout and perform some test bakes ready for the big competition tomorrow. I know how important this opportunity is for you all.'

'Important?' repeated Mr Ross as seemed to be his habit. 'It's not important, Mr Crystal. It's life changing. If the winner is awarded the contract with Bentley Brothers, they'll never worry about money again as long as they live. Never mind the cash prize, Mr Crystal, it's the contract we are all here for.'

Another man, this one wearing all black, decided to join the argument, but he wasn't against the event organiser like the others, he was against his baking opponents. 'Still moaning are you, Ross? Perhaps you should pack up early and leave before you waste your time tomorrow.' To his right stood another man, tall and skinny with youthful versions of his father's features, the name on his black tunic was Oliver's Bakery, Wetherby.

Mr Ross's face twitched in annoyance. 'See what I mean, Mr Crystal? This man's Yorkshire puddings are a joke compared to mine.' Mr Ross turned his head to yell across the marquee. 'Aiden! bring the puddings lad!'

They were forced to wait, but only for a few seconds as a young man came running with a tray of Yorkshire puddings.

'Look at these, will thee?' bragged Mr Ross. 'How is anyone going to beat these?'

Albert eyed the Yorkshire puddings, which were probably the highest he had ever seen. They were towering, crisp, and golden.

Mr Ross jabbed a finger at his rival from Oliver's Bakery. 'Yet he feels he can win and is confident enough to taunt me. It's not right, I tell thee.'

Alan raised both his hands in a gesture of supplication. 'Please, gentlemen, and lady,' he added quickly, remembering the woman present. 'Everyone enters the competition with an equal chance of victory. The puddings will be judged on the same set of criteria: crispness, rise, flavour, and colour. The heats are to be judged by me, but the final, which I can assure you, you all have an equal chance of reaching, will be judged by a panel. There is no way to cheat the panel of judges. The puddings will be baked in full view of the audience and event staff. The winner of each heat will progress to the final and will get another chance to bake for the grand prize. There are, of course, other trophies up for grabs, so if you are lacking confidence you can enter the sweet treat contest or compete for the most innovative dish. I hear there haven't been many entries for the decorative dish contest yet, perhaps you should all think about vying for a chance to scoop that prize.' Alan span the suggestion as if it were something really worthy of winning, but the contestants stared at him like he were being a fool.

'Stuff and nonsense, Mr Crystal,' growled Mr Ross. 'No Yorkshireman worth his salt would waste time making fancy shapes with Yorkshire puddings. I'll win first place, you mark my word, Mr Crystal. You too, Oliver.' He poked a finger at his opponent in black. 'My family's Yorkies have been winning awards and prizes for generations.'

Mr Oliver's smile remained in place. 'Good luck then,' he taunted. It was an open challenge, but not the first one delivered in the last few minutes. If Albert expected friendly rivalry between the competing teams, he was to be disappointed because the undercurrent of cut-throat competitiveness threatened to boil over.

Still glaring at each other, the teams drifted back to the competition area, another raised platform with barriers around it to keep tomorrow's spectators at bay.

Moving away from the baking competition, which took up most of the left-hand wing of the marquee, Albert and Gary, led by Alan were now facing the area reserved for the record attempt where a large, open food

41

preparation area sat beneath a banner telling visitors they were witnessing the world largest Yorkshire pudding being made. A row of giant machines, looking a lot like oversized cement mixers, were arranged in a line with a raised platform around them so the bakers could get the ingredients in.

Moving around in the food preparation area, which had a barrier from which visitors could watch, Albert saw perhaps a dozen bakers. They all wore white jackets beneath white chef's hats. The trousers were a grey and black check pattern. There was a rhythm to their work which proceeded with minimal chatter and under the watchful gaze of a tall and burly man.

'They're just doing some test baking today,' Alan explained. 'To qualify, the world record breaking pudding has to be cooked all over and be edible.'

'How big are they attempting to make it?' Gary asked.

Alan's eyes flared with excitement, but he didn't answer. Instead, he backed toward the wall of the marquee and waved his arm as a signal to look outside. Indulging him, Albert and Gary came closer and looked through the plastic panel window of the canvas building.

Beaming with joy and excitement, Alan bragged, 'It's to be fifty-five yards long. That will smash the previous record.'

'It's a monstrosity!' The comment came from behind them, as once again, Brian put in an appearance. 'This is not what our championships is about. That's why in the entire history of the championships, there has never been anything like this before.'

Alan wasn't to be put off. 'Think of all the publicity it will bring, Brian. The television is going to be here tomorrow. York will attract an extra million tourists next year just because of this. Think of the revenue to the local economy.'

'Gawdy and unnecessary,' spat Brian.

'The mayor didn't think so,' Alan returned with a smile because he'd already won their fight.

The cat did not appear to have moved since Rex last saw him. 'Do your feet work, cat? Or are you just so lazy that you let your human carry you everywhere?'

The cat was lying on its side, the paws on its right side hanging loosely down into free space over Brian's arm. It lifted its front paw now to slowly lick it and rub behind its ear. 'You're a dog,' it replied languidly. 'Such concepts are beyond your comprehension. Your place is on the floor, scrabbling for scraps and dancing to your human's tune. Cats are above humans, that is why I am carried about. It's a form of worship, you see.'

Rex was just about ready to pounce. One good leap would get him close enough that the cat would climb its human's face and learn a little humility on the way. Stupid human, carrying a cat around. Lunging might pull his own human over though. Rex was conscious that his human was old and not all that good at getting up once he was down. It was probably best to wait for another opportunity, so he bit his rising bile down and closed his eyes to the cat's comments.

'Hey, dog!' the cat called. 'Fetch me a bone!'

Rex's eyes snapped open. His feet were already moving as he stomped on the gas and committed to his decision. The lead was hanging loosely in Albert's hand, not looped around his wrist as it so often was and whipped free without yanking his arm. This was a mercy because he wasn't even looking in the right direction and might have dislocated his arm had he attempted to hold Rex back.

The cat saw the dog coming and knew it had gone too far. 'Time to go,' it mewled, scrambling to get purchase on Brian's jacket. Brian hadn't paid the dog any attention until it moved, but now his cat, Mr Fluffikins was shredding his jacket as he ran upward over his shoulder and leapt from his back.

Shouting, 'Catch me if you can, mutt!' the cat landed with his legs already sprinting.

Rex barked something unprintable in response and barrelled forward. Brian was in his way but there was a gap to go around him. Rex dove for it, but Brian, in a state of panic, chose to go that way to avoid the dog and thus presented his shins to the dog's granite-like skull.

All Albert, Gary, and Alan could do was watch in horror as Rex used Brian's legs like a giant cat flap. One moment Brian was standing upright, the next he was two feet off the floor and parallel to it. He crashed back down to Earth with an 'Ooooff' of exhaled air, the space beneath him devoid of dog because Rex was long gone.

The cat, far smaller, just as fast, and twice as nimble, even though it was a bit on the podgy side, was going under objects to avoid the dog. Fuelled by anger and imbued with a sense of divine retribution for all dogkind, Rex just went through the obstacles the cat went under.

'I'm gonna get you, cat!' Rex barked loudly.

The people in the marquee: chefs, caterers, delivery men, and the people still setting things up, all turned to see the kerfuffle. The cat appeared, leaping onto a table to avoid the dog, and running full pelt along it. The table was being set out for a display of Yorkshire-made pickles and preserves, the stallholder standing back to see how it looked when the cat flew along it. The woman shrieked in fear, but Fluffikins leapt the carefully arranged tower of strawberry jams, landing safely on the other side, not one jar broken. The woman put one hand to her heart and the other on the table to support herself in relief.

Rex went through the stall like a freight train.

From his vantage point, Albert could only cringe. He'd tried shouting for Rex to return but he knew it was a worthless gesture. Gary and Alan were attempting to help Brian back to his feet though he angrily slapped their hands away.

'Get off me!' he demanded. 'Let me go! I told you to get that dog out of here. He's far too big to be allowed inside. You've already ruined the championship, Alan,' he made a point of sneering the event organiser's name, 'and it hasn't even started yet!'

'Are you bleeding, sir?' asked Gary, genuine concern on his face. He could see the spreading stain on Brian's jacket and hoped he wasn't really hurt.

Brian tracked Gary's eyes to find the same mark and threw his hands in his air. 'Oh, well, that's just perfect. On top of everything else. Your stupid dog has ruined my jacket.'

'Is that blood, sir? Are you hurt?' Gary repeated.

Brian's expression changed, a shadow of doubt creeping onto his face momentarily. It was gone in a flash as he said, 'What? Err, no. This is just … it's um … it's cough medicine. Yes, it's cough medicine. I have a tickly throat, so I picked some up on the way here today.' His explanation given; the look of righteous indignation swiftly returned. 'Now, if you don't mind. I think I will collect my cat.'

Alan had the cough medicine on his fingers from helping Brian to his feet. He took a handkerchief from his pocket, shaking it out to unfold it before attempting to wipe his hand clean.

The cat was, at that point, balanced on top of a pallet of flour which was still loaded onto a forklift truck. The far end of the marquee was pinned open so supplies for the world record attempt could be brought in.

Getting up there had been easy enough, the cat used his claws to scale the paper sacks and in so doing, had ripped most of them open. A small avalanche of flour had mounded onto the floor and was all over Rex as he continued to try to get to the cat.

Loosely translated, his barks were, 'How long do you think you can stay up there, cat?' I give you the loose translation because Rex was, by this point, using some fairly inventive cursing to punctuate his sentences.

The cat adopted a cat pose, lifting one lazy paw into the air to lick it while sitting on his hindquarters as if there was nothing in the world which could possibly bother it. 'I shall come down shortly, dog. By then you will have been clipped back onto your lead and taken away like the dumb beast you are.' Then, with a flick of his tail, the cat locked eyes with the dog ten feet below. 'Ooh, I wonder if they will put your excitable nature down to still … you know, having your bits. Maybe it's time Rex went to get his trousers lightened; don't you think?'

What the cat hadn't counted on was the team of bakers drafted into make the giant Yorkshire pudding taking offense as the cat destroyed their provisions.

Albert, Gary, and Alan were all hustling to get to the scene of the next drama. Between the shouts of the bakers, Rex's barking, and the cat hissing at everyone and everything, Alan's attempt at calling for calm went unheard.

In a bid to get the undamaged bags of flour out of the way of the dog, who was himself now covered in white powder, one of the bakers jumped into the seat of the forklift and began pulling levers. That he didn't know which lever did what became instantly apparent when the pallet of flour flew upward into the air.

Cries of alarm rang out as it wobbled ten feet above the marquee floor. Rex knew well enough to abandon his quest for the cat, sent a silent prayer the feline would get squashed flat and ran for his life.

The baker at the forklift controls had eyes the size of saucers now, his hands twitching as he tried to decipher which lever might do what. All around him, though none daring to come forward to help, other bakers shouted instructions. Their voices competed and conflicted though, no two people telling him the same thing.

Albert grabbed Gary's arm to hold him back. 'Best we don't get too close, lad.'

Too late though, the load, already unstable, pitched over as the cat decided it was time to seek safer ground. His leap proved to be the final straw as fifty-pound bags of flour began to topple from the leading edge of the pallet. The first one started a cascade as more and more fell from the lopsided pallet. Each gathered sufficient speed on its way to the floor that they exploded on impact, sending up an ever-expanding cloud of fine white powder. Still running, Rex felt sure he was clear of the danger, until one sack fell from the left side of the high pallet onto the end of a table, flipping the other end into the air. On the table had been caterer size cartons of milk, open because they were about to be used.

The cloud of flour continued to expand, engulfing all in its path. It was scary enough to make Albert decide Rex would have to fend for himself.

'Get to the doors!' yelled Gary, opting to save himself from the floury storm heading their way. 'Every man for himself!'

Gary and Alan vanished from sight and Brian was nowhere to be seen. Albert knew he was never going to make it: the entrance doors were too far away. He wasn't up to running either, so he fished his handkerchief from his pocket and held it over his mouth. He would find his way out and do his best to keep the flour from invading his respiratory system until he did.

'Come on, Dad!' yelled Gary, yanking him through a side flap and out of the marquee a few seconds before a billowing cloud of flour tried to follow them.

Alan was out of breath and had his hands pressed to the side of his head. 'Oh, my goodness. What a disaster. However are we going to clean this up in time?'

Albert thought it a small mercy Brian wasn't with them. Guessing he must have chosen a different exit since he wasn't around to stick the knife into their host. To their left, twenty or more bakers and stallholders were doing the same thing as Alan: gawping through the plastic windows of the marquee. They couldn't see anything – the whole inside was just a fog of pure white.

With a fresh escape of flour, the flap Albert escaped through moved to one side, and from the mess trudged a defeated and sorry-looking German Shepherd. His fur was slick with a rudimentary batter as the flying milk landed all around him as he ran, splashing his flour impregnated coat with liquid which was very quickly absorbed by the dry ingredient.

All Albert could do was stare. 'My goodness, Rex. I don't think Mrs Morton will let you back into our bed and breakfast looking like that.'

Rex hung his head. 'I hate cats.'

Poor Alan was bordering on catatonic looking at the mess and gibbering over and over about the clean-up operation just to get it back to a state where they could begin to prepare for the next day.

'There's a bigger problem,' offered Gary, getting Alan's attention.

'A bigger problem than this?' the event organiser choked.

Gary nodded sadly. 'All that airborne flour will settle, but not for a while. Until it does, you are looking at a big risk of explosion.' Albert's eyes flared at the very real possibility his son was right. He'd seen the fresh hazard before anyone else had thought of it. Gary was backing away from the marquee, taking out his phone only once he'd got some distance from it. Albert doubted the phone would be able to set off a flour explosion, but better safe than sorry.

The fire brigade would have to wash the surfaces down and blast the flour out to the drains. Albert looked at Rex again, the dog looking more like a German Shepherd shaped donut ready to go in the fryer than anything else. 'They can wash you off too,' he said.

Rex didn't like the sound of that, but he was distracted by Alan saying, 'I don't feel too good.' Albert looked his way, just in time to see the museum curator throw up. The term 'throw up' fails, however, to come close to capturing the projectile vomiting they bore witness too. Describing it later, Albert would refer to it as akin to a magic trick where the magician performed a spell to empty a human being. Watching him from a few yards away, and wishing he were in a different county, Albert expected Alan to deflate like a balloon as everything the man had ever eaten made a break for freedom on the grass outside the marquee.

When it was done, Alan wiped his mouth and looked about with an apologetic look. Then he collapsed.

Gary was too far away to do anything about Alan collapsing, but he got to see it and into his phone he sighed, 'You'd better add an ambulance.'

Albert couldn't work out what to be most concerned about, his dog, the venue for the World Yorkshire Pudding Competition, or the man now groaning on the floor. When, in the next breath, Alan went floppy and lifeless, the decision became easy.

Gary was already running in Alan's direction and got there before Albert. By the time the sirens could be heard approaching – the second time in a few hours Albert had the emergency services to his location – Alan was stable, but wishing he wasn't conscious.

First to arrive was the fire brigade, the same bunch as earlier, who were filled with amusement to see Rex again. 'Does he often get into trouble like this?' asked Station Officer Hamilton with an amused twinkle in his eyes.

Albert let his shoulders slump as he gave a sad nod. 'Yes, all the time.'

Rex was thoroughly unhappy with his current situation. Large chunks of his coat were matted together with the flour and milk mix which was beginning to solidify. It was heavy and it didn't taste very nice when he tried chewing it out. Also, he had already heard the word 'bath' several times and couldn't see a way to avoid it.

The paramedics arrived at a run, bringing their gear with them in heavy bags they carried on straps over their shoulders. They took over tending to Alan which allowed Gary to check on his father.

'Is this what you had planned?' he asked flippantly.

Albert huffed a laugh. 'I wonder if they will get this all turned around in time.' They were sitting on a low wall, looking in through the now open sides of the marquee. The firefighters were washing the flour out, but it didn't look as bad as it had initially. Most of the stall holders and attractions were yet to be set up. If they could wash the flour away, and let the surfaces dry overnight, maybe none of the visitors and competitors would even know the difference.

The sound of the hoses blasting away at the flour dropped as one by one Station Officer Hamilton ordered them turned off. He was heading inside to see how much more needed to be done, but the sudden drop in background noise allowed everyone to hear the argument raging between the bakers and Brian.

'Are you out of your mind?' shouted a large man with beefy arms and a pink hairnet keeping his dark locks in place. It was the same man Albert saw overseeing the work in the record attempt area earlier. His face was bright red with anger as he shouted down at the smaller man. The baker had the advantage of having a dozen other bakers, men and women, on his side. They had formed a wall of support, surrounding him on either side with every set of eyes expressing the same negative emotion toward the tiny man.

'I don't care what you say,' snapped Brian, uncowed by size or numbers. 'The record attempt is off. With Alan Crystal incapacitated, the running of this year's show defaults to me, where it should always have been. So, I'm sorry but there will be no ridiculous, gawdy, and ultimately probably failed attempt to break a pointless world record no one cares about.'

'Will we get paid?' asked a quiet voice. Albert strained his eyes and ears to see who had spoken. The voice, a woman's, sounded familiar but her face was lost among everyone else.

The beefy man was barely keeping his rage in check which drew Gary's attention. There were fire and ambulance services present, but no police which meant he was the only person on the scene responsible for keeping the peace. Reluctantly, but accepting that intervening now might save bloodshed, he started in their direction, reaching for his police identification as he went.

Following Gary, Albert caught the beefy man's next response. 'Are you going to stop us then? Are you, little man?' He was eighteen inches taller and at least a hundred pounds heavier than Brian. To accentuate his point, he jabbed a meaty finger down into Brian's upper chest driving him back a foot. Bending from the waist to growl into the short man's face, he said, 'You so much as try it, and I'll stuff you into the mixer and turn you into one of the puddings.'

Another voice jumped into the fray. 'Yeah, what about all the money that's been spent? What about all the advertising? People are coming here just to see it!' Unlike the beefy man's voice, the new voice was using reason and calm and all eyes swung to see a woman stepping away from the leading edge of the gang of bakers. 'Mr Pumphrey, so much effort has been put into this project. You have to let us go ahead now.'

Gary allowed his pace to slow, the tension in the group was weakening; maybe he wouldn't have to step in after all.

When the woman added the word, 'Please,' in a pleading voice, she handed all the power to Brian. He could say no, but he would appear pathetic and petty were he to do so.

Instead, Brian took a pace back, and sneered at the group of bakers, 'Go ahead. Fail miserably if you must. Good luck finding fresh ingredients in time.' Spinning on his heel, he stomped away across the damp grass.

As he left the scene, Station Officer Hamilton came back into view. He was returning from inside the marquee and heading for the bakers. 'You can go back inside now if you wish; there's no danger.

Wordlessly, the bakers began to drift in the direction of the marquee. They had equipment to sort out, their ingredients were undoubtedly ruined, and they were seriously short on time if they were going to break a world record tomorrow.

The beefy man was still glaring at the back of Brian's skull as he sauntered away. His trembling lips could barely contain the insult hidden behind them, but just when Albert thought the large man might sling it and undo what the calm voice of the woman had achieved, she touched his arm. The large man stiffened, but when he saw it was her, he glanced about and pulled her into a swift hug. They didn't hold it for long, probably worried about people commenting on their public display of affection. There was a very quick peck on the lips before they just as swiftly parted and pretended to not be doing anything.

The couple, now standing a yard or more apart, started to move toward the marquee, but Station Officer Hamilton held out a hand to stop them.

'I have a question about your flour.'

Beefy's feet stopped moving just as they were getting started. 'The flour?'

A minute later, all the bakers, plus Albert and Gary, were standing around the remaining sacks of flour. The firefighters had noticed something when they were washing the spilt flour across the floor and out of the marquee. Parts of it were not washing away, not the way flour should.

It didn't take much to work out what it was they were seeing: The flour had been cut with salt.

'Why?' asked Beefy.

'Better yet, who?' corrected the woman Albert saw the beefy man kiss.

Bath Time

His human had clipped his lead back to his collar and handed him off to three firefighters. Rex then had to watch his human back away, saying, 'Sorry, Rex,' just before he turned around.

'Sorry?' questioned Rex, his head down and his ears flopping sadly to the sides. 'Me too. If I ever catch that cat ...'

'What have we here?' asked one of the firefighters. Rex remembered them from earlier when he was lost, and they brought him back to his human. Normally, he would be pleased to see people he recognised but not under these circumstances. They were going to get him wet and, worse yet, soapy. He hated being soapy. It always went in his nose and his coat then smelled weird for days. He would always try to normalise the smell by finding things to roll in, yet inexplicable, as he attempted to rid himself of the awful soap smell, his human would yell at him to stop. On several occasions, when he'd found something that would truly mask the soap smell, his human then bathed him again. It made no sense at all.

He always fought against getting a bath, but not this time: he knew he had to get the matted gunk out of his fur, and he couldn't do it by himself. It tasted salty for a start – really salty, like the time his human left the shopping unattended and the first thing Rex stole turned out to be a box of sea salt crystals. The taste had stayed with him for days.

The three humans around him were discussing how best to tackle his dilemma. He didn't bother to pay any attention to what they were saying: it was all bad news. They came at him with a hose first. They took off his assistance dog harness and once his coat was wet, another of them started to apply a pinkish detergent. He didn't like the smell but it was better than some soaps he'd had to suffer.

Shutting out the experience and going to his happy place; the one where he got to chew a large bone while lying on a bed of squirrel mafia he'd recently triumphed over. He tried to focus on the taste of the imaginary bone, but the sound of the cat laughing cut through his daydream. Snapping his eyes open once more, he spotted the cat. Unlike him, there wasn't a trace of flour on its fur.

'Dogs,' the cat muttered, idly licking a paw, and wiping it around his ear. 'So graceful, so lithe, so elegant. Wait, no, that's cats, isn't it? Dogs are little more than noise covered in dirt.'

Rex, despite having two set of hands on him lathering his coat with soapy suds, elected to kill the cat. The firefighters had positioned him so he was standing on all four paws, which made the transition from stationary to running a simple one.

However, the firefighters were not new to this game and had pinned his lead to the ground. Rex threw his weight forward, startling all three firefighters, but just as he left their hands on a straight-line trajectory to moggy murder, his lead reached its limit and his head stopped moving. There being nothing to equal out the kinetic energy of his forward thrust, his body spun around on the end of his lead to splat back down on the wet grass.

Ignoring the pain coming from his neck where his collar bit in, and from his hip where it hit the ground, Rex twisted around to curse the cat. Mr Fluffikins was no longer where he had been because his human had picked him up again.

'Where did you get to, you naughty cat?' cooed the cat's human. 'Oh, I can't stay mad at you, you are just too gorgeous.' The human was making kissy noises and stroking the cat's head.

Rex was about to get back to his feet and bark his rage once more, but a whiff of something caught his nose and caused him to stop. He concentrated, drawing in a deep noseful of air which he held. Closing his eyes, he blocked out everything else and searched his memory. He knew the smell and it turned his stomach. It was coming from the cat's human but hadn't been there before. It was new, suggesting the human must have come into contact with it recently.

When he opened his eyes again, the cat and his human were gone, and the three firefighters were picking Rex up to finish the job of cleaning him. Obediently, though the cold water was beginning to penetrate the inner layer of his coat, he stood and let them finish the job. His canine brain generally thought in straight lines; conspiracy and intricately woven plots were beyond him. It had never stopped him from working out who the bad guy was though and there was something about the scent he just detected that tripped a switch in his head.

He would need to tell his human about it.

That it was salt got challenged and confirmed by only two of the bakers who refused to believe it and chose to dab their fingers in the crystals. Their opinion was sufficient to convince everyone else. The pallet of flour that had been on the forklift truck had not survived the ordeal of the marquee being washed down, but they had plenty more of it stored outside. They would have to open every bag to know if they were all the same, but it seemed likely they were.

Beefy, who appeared to be either the boss or just a spokesperson, said, 'We'll order new. Right now. And we'll collect it ourselves.'

'Who's going to pay for that?' wailed a ginger-haired man in the same baker's white jacket and checked trousers. 'I don't think the venue is going to stump up the extra cash with that horrible midget Pumphrey in charge now.'

Beefy hadn't thought of that, but while his eyes darted wildly about and he tried to stay on top of the situation, he said, 'I'll pay. At least … I've got a little set aside.' He looked panicked suddenly, as if he'd blurted his initial response about paying for fifty-five yards worth of ingredients and was only now thinking about what that might cost.

'I can put some money up,' volunteered the calm woman. She was looking around at the rest of the bakers. 'Come on guys. We've been practicing this. We can do it and get our names in the record books, or we can go home and accept we just wasted our time.'

Albert figured her appeal was supposed to generate support and get people putting their hands in their pockets. It didn't. About half the bakers present threw their hands in the air as they made excuses and some even started directly for the door. It was then, as the press of chefs parted, that Albert saw a face he recognised. It was the one he heard ask about getting paid but then couldn't spot.

'I'll cover the costs,' he said before he realised he was saying it.

'Dad?' Gary questioned, not sure he had heard his father correctly.

The words were in the air though, and in the ears of everyone present. He couldn't take it back, the innocent eyes staring at him across the marquee wouldn't let him.

The baby was in his mother's arms again, but now Rosie was clad in chef's whites and checked trousers. Albert had no idea how much this was going to cost him, but it was going to be less than he had languishing in the bank and would give him a sense of value he couldn't get spending his money anywhere else.

In a louder voice, he said, 'I'll cover the costs.' What he didn't say was that he was also going to find out who tampered with the ingredients. Alan, who was still being treated by the paramedics, said the Yorkshire pudding needed to be edible or pass some kind of taste in order to qualify for the record which meant this was a deliberate attempt to scupper the teams' attempt.

Gary got within touching distance of his father's shoulder. 'Are you sure about this, Pops?'

Albert was yet to break eye contact with Rosie's baby, but he nodded. 'Sure enough.' In his mind, it was already done, yet possibly it still wasn't enough, though he wasn't sure why he felt like that. Rosie was sad; she didn't have the life she wanted – maybe she deserved better, but that wasn't reason enough to come rushing to her aid.

Albert nodded his head. 'I came here to make a Yorkshire pudding, son. Now I get to make the biggest one ever. I can't put a value on that.' The bakers who had been heading for the doors were all turning around now and coming back. Those nearer, were coming toward Albert showing smiles of thanks as they crowded around him like he was the messiah. It was far too late to retract his offer, and he had no desire to do so. What he did feel a need to do was investigate what had been happening.

Alan, the chief judge and organiser of this event was attacked a few hours ago and there was something wrong about that too. Albert had been biding his time, trying to find an appropriate point in their conversation to ask about the money he saw and why Alan failed to mention it to the police. He saw what he saw – the mugger had gone for the briefcase and Alan had almost let him have it. Had it not been for Rex, the mugger would have got away with however much cash was in the briefcase, but a few hours on, Alan appeared to be suffering from a different kind of attack. Were it not for the failed mugging, Albert would assume the man had simply fallen ill, but given the spectacular and sudden manner in which the sickness occurred, he was willing to bet this was somehow linked to the earlier incident.

Whatever the case, Alan was about to go to hospital and when Albert added to that the possibility that the bakers' ingredients had been deliberately targeted, it meant someone was up to no good.

All this swirled around inside Albert's head until it was abruptly stopped by his right hand getting crushed. Several of the bakers had chosen to shake his hand, but Beefy's turn resulted in the bones in his hand all getting mashed together.

'We shall have to get you a set of whites,' he cheered, pumping Albert's right arm up and down. 'You will join in tomorrow, won't you?'

Albert hid his wince when he got his hand back, forcing a smile as he rubbed his right hand with his left to make sure it wasn't mangled. 'Yes, of course. Thank you. It would be an honour to take part. I must warn you though, I'm not much of a baker.'

'That won't matter,' Beefy assured him.

His girlfriend/wife, a woman in her forties standing just to Beefy's left echoed his sentiment, 'Yes, we'll look after you. Thank you so much for rescuing us.'

It was a day for rescuing people it seemed. Albert suddenly had a lot of names to learn, and it was just then that he noticed they all had their names stitched into their clothing over the right breast where a name badge might usually hang. He had to step back to get Beefy's into focus and almost choked when he read what it said.

'Beefy?'

Beefy dropped his eyes to his name tag and laughed. 'Yes, that's what everyone calls me. My last name is Botham, and well ...' He didn't need to explain any further, Albert remembered the famous cricket player Ian 'Beefy' Botham.

'I'm Suzalls,' said Beefy's girlfriend/wife.

'And I'm Rosie,' said Rosie. 'And this is Teddy.'

Albert turned his attention to the sad-looking young woman holding her baby. 'How is your hand?' he asked.

Rosie glanced down at it and back up. 'It's sore, but I don't have time to be injured. I need this work.'

Albert nodded his acknowledgement but didn't pry into her business. To have something to say, he said, 'I am glad I was able to help out.'

Teddy chose that moment to fart loudly and then giggle. It startled Albert, nursing his own children was so far in the past now, he'd all but forgotten how gassy they could be. Rosie's cheeks coloured as everyone within earshot turned her way and burst out laughing. She had to laugh too, kissing her son's head, and apologising to everyone.

Beefy clapped his hands together. 'Right. I guess we'd better get on with it then.' The bakers busied themselves with various duties, tidying up and sorting out. Their food prep area was soaked and there were ruined ingredients everywhere plus trashed batter mix in the row of giant machines. Albert heard Beefy and others discussing the need to have people in over night to prepare the amount of batter required. To make the amount they needed required hundreds of loads to go through the machines. They were then being loaded into hoppers outside which would hold the batter until it was ready for the pour.

Gary asked, 'What are you up to, Dad?'

Albert wriggled his lips from side to side as he thought. 'There's something going on here, Gary.'

Gary didn't bother to hide his exasperated expression. 'Yes, Dad, there's a Yorkshire pudding competition and world record attempt. That's what is going on.'

Albert cut his eyes at his son. 'I think I'll check on our new friend, Alan.' With that, he left the tent. He needed to find Rex anyway.

Poisoned?

Outside, the paramedics were packing up. Alan was loaded onto a stretcher, but due to the uneven terrain, the wheels were not extended, and the firefighters were chipping in to help carry him to the ambulance more than a hundred yards away in the road.

Albert wanted to intercept them, but Rex had seen him and was haring his way. Small droplets of water were flying from his coat as he ran. The firefighters had declared him clean. Or, more accurately, as clean as they were going to get him. They used some old towels they kept in the truck to dry his fur as best they could and had then encouraged him to perform shuttle sprints between them to eject more of the water. Rex happily complied, chasing the improvised towel tied in a knot as the firefighters gamely threw it. That was until the scent of his human reached his nostrils. At that point, he made an abrupt right turn and ran to greet the one human he genuinely trusted.

'The cat's human smells of something he shouldn't,' Rex announced, skidding to a stop on the soggy grass in a shower of wet dirt which coated the bottom of Albert's shoes and the hem of his trousers.

'Oh, dog,' sighed Albert. 'I think you just got yourself all muddy again. 'Come on, quickly, I need to speak to the paramedics before they take Alan away.'

One of the firefighters was approaching with Rex's lead, which they'd removed so the dog could run around. It meant Albert ought to wait for the man to arrive, but the paramedics were leaving so he needed to chase after them and he wasn't exactly a racing snake these days. Caught in a moment of indecision, he grabbed Gary's sleeve.

'Son can you get the paramedics to hold on for thirty seconds?'

Rex said, 'I don't think you heard me. I said the cat's human is up to something. He doesn't smell right, and I don't mean just because he is one of those truly strange humans who likes to spend time with a cat.'

Gary, ignoring the noises his dad's dog was making, frowned at his father. 'Why do you want me to stop the paramedics?'

Albert had to glance down at his dog, who was looking up at him with an expectant face as if waiting for a response, then at the firefighter, who was now paused half way to him while another firefighter shouted something to him about what they were doing next. Then he risked a glance at the paramedics who were about to vanish from sight around the edge of the marquee on their way back to the ambulance, and finally to his son who was still just staring back at him with a questioning look on his face.

Frustrated, he said a colourful word he rarely used in public and started after the paramedics. Turning his body slightly, as the firefighter, Rex, and Gary gave him confused eyes, he said, 'Gary, please collect Rex's lead and thank the nice firefighters for me. Rex, with me.'

Rex needed no further encouragement, dashing after his human to catch him in a few easy bounds. It was turning out to be an odd sort of day, but they were together, and it looked like his human had got the message about the cat's human. 'Are we going to get them then? Are we going to investigate the cat's human and the cat? Can we arrange to have them put in a nice jail cell together somewhere? I wonder if cats get their fur shaved when they go to the big house?'

Albert looked down at Rex. His dog was bouncing about on his paws like a puppy might – brimming with energy and unable to contain it. He was also making lots of chuffing noises, trying to impart a message of some kind which Albert's ears were not able to translate.

By the time they got to the road, the paramedics had loaded Alan into the back of the ambulance and were about to shut the doors.

'Hello?' called Albert, shuffling along as fast as he could. 'Hello?' His second call was a little louder and got one of the paramedics to look his way. 'Sorry, I'm sure you are just about to rush off. Can I ask what is wrong with Alan? He's a dear friend,' Albert stretched the truth to breaking point, 'and he looks so terribly ill all of a sudden.'

The paramedics shut the doors, one of them going inside to tend to the patient, as the other started moving around to the driver's door. He didn't run, and even sort of crab-walked sideways so he could answer Albert's question.

'We're not sure what has happened to him. It might be that he has ingested a toxin of some kind. You say you're his friend: what has he eaten recently?'

Albert didn't know the answer to that question. 'I only joined him after lunch, I'm afraid,' he admitted. 'You think he might have been poisoned?' he paraphrased what the paramedic told him.

The sentence, structured that way, gave the paramedic cause to pause halfway into his seat. 'Poisoned? Possibly, but the way you said it makes it sound like a deliberate act. I'm not suggesting that, only that he might have accidentally ingested something. Lots of everyday products contain toxins such as cyanide or arsenic in small amounts.' He grabbed the door, making it obvious he intended to shut it. 'Excuse me now, I have to go.'

Albert stepped back a pace, allowing the ambulance driver to close his door. A heartbeat later, the ambulance pulled away, the lights on top already flashing. Both he and Rex stared at the taillights as it departed but when it moved, it revealed the other side of the street where a large man with no neck and a leather jacket was standing.

66

Albert's eyes bugged right out, surprise propelling his feet forward as he shouted, 'Hey!'

He stepped into the street, intending to confront the man. This was the third time Albert had seen him which was too many for it to be a coincidence. His right arm went taut suddenly, yanking him backward just as a screech of brakes sounded to his left.

A car skidded to a stop right where Albert would have been if Rex hadn't pulled him back. The driver shouted something unpleasant before stomping on his accelerator again leaving Albert to cool his racing pulse. 'Thanks, pal,' he patted Rex's skull. 'You saved me there.'

As expected, when Albert looked, the man in the black leather jacket was gone. Seeing him three times made Albert want to know who he was and what connected him to the event. Who could he ask though?

Traipsing back to the marquee, Albert and Rex were thinking very different thoughts. Albert was troubled by Alan's condition. The possibility that it was brought about by the ingestion of a toxin bothered him – he didn't think it was accidental for one moment. The man had been inexplicably attacked just a few hours ago and had then lied about the event to the police, playing it down as a random mugging. Albert's decision to leave it and enjoy the weekend with his son had been the right one to make at the time; or so it seemed. However, now the same man was on his way to hospital and Albert couldn't help but question if intervening earlier might have prevented things getting this far. Who was the young man with the baton? Was it the same person who then poisoned him? Then there was still the question of the bakers' ingredients and whether they had been deliberately messed with.

By his human's feet, Rex wasn't thinking about the man in the ambulance at all. He'd worked out what the smell was. Not that he had a name for it. He'd come across it once before as a police dog. When he was still little more than a puppy in training, he'd snuck into the storeroom they kept the kibble in and eaten his fill. His fill turned out to be rather more than he ought to have ingested, and more than his stomach could hold. It resulted in a visit from the vet and some medicine to make him regurgitate everything he'd ever eaten – or so it seemed. The memory still haunted him and the smell of the medicine they gave him remained ingrained in his olfactory system forever. He'd just smelled it again on the cat's human.

Gary found his dad still standing in the street with the dog sitting obediently by his side. 'What are you up to, Dad?'

Albert heard his son clip the lead back onto Rex's collar but didn't bother to look his way when he replied, 'There's no coincidence in policework, son.'

A snort of laughter escaped Gary's lips. 'That again? I would be inclined to agree with you, Dad, but we are not doing police work. We were supposed to be exploring York, having a couple of drinks and some food, and then learning to bake a perfect Yorkshire pudding. Now we, or rather you, seem to be caught up in a world record attempt which you are paying for – goodness only knows what that is going to cost – and you want to add to that what … investigating something? What is it that you think might be going on here, Dad? It's a baking competition in a Yorkshire city. Or are we back on your criminal mastermind conspiracy nonsense?'

Albert found his son's choice of words rather harsh. There was no need to call it nonsense. Something was occurring here; he didn't know what it was, not yet at least, but his detective brain wouldn't rest until he dug a little deeper. Saying that now or saying what he thought of his son's inability to see the clues he found blatantly obvious would only put a dampener on the weekend, so he bit them down.

Turning around to face Gary, Albert extended his hand to take the dog lead, and said, 'It's getting late. We seem to have used up quite a chunk of the day what with one thing and another. How about we wrap things up here, make sure the bakers can buy the ingredients they need, and then find ourselves a watering hole somewhere so we can taste the region's local ales?' He delivered his suggestion with an encouraging smile. Maybe

Gary couldn't see the same clues. Maybe Gary didn't want to. Albert knew his son was involved in policework all day every day and might just need to have a break from chasing criminals. Albert would poke his nose around later - the bakers said they would need to be here all night.

Relief washed across Gary's face; his father was seeing sense finally. 'Okay, Dad, that sounds like a great plan. Are you sure you want to spend all that money on the crazy giant Yorkshire pudding?'

Albert started walking back toward the marquee, shrugging his shoulders as he went. 'I can't take it with me. You lot don't need it all; there'll be plenty from the sale of the house. Besides, we don't know how much it will be yet.'

As it turned out, it was more than he thought, but not so much that it made him want to change his mind. Beefy had been looking for him and didn't hide his relief when Albert reappeared; they had thought him to have changed his mind and made a swift exit.

The order to the caterer had been placed, it simply required payment so they could collect it. 'Charlie and Rosco will have to take their van,' Beefy explained. 'It's after delivery hours now and I didn't want to spend more of your money paying the out of hours delivery fee.'

'That was good of you,' replied Albert, wondering what Petunia, his wonderful wife would have made of his latest eccentric idea. He still missed her dearly but a year after losing her, he was able to form her into his thoughts without feeling a stab of pain each time he did. 'How many of you will be working through the night?' Albert asked.

Beefy started pointing people out. 'I'm staying on now with Rosco, Charlie, and Mavis. Then at midnight, Dave, Dave, Dave, and Rosie will be back to take over.'

'Rosie?' questioned Albert, ignoring that they had three men with the same first name all on the same shift. 'What about her baby?'

Beefy shrugged. 'She volunteered. Most of us work for Uncle Bert's but she's a local hire and still to prove herself.'

Albert's forehead concertinaed onto itself. He knew who Uncle Bert's were: a giant firm who held the top position in the pre-cooked and frozen market for Yorkshire puddings and other foods. 'If this is being run by Uncle Bert's, how come you're not wearing their logo? Better yet, why am I paying for replacement ingredients?'

'Ah,' said Beefy. 'Uncle Bert's isn't behind this. They wouldn't even give us the time off. We had to take our own time. Uncle Bert's hold the world record. That's why they won't support our attempt. The mayor's office approached them directly; it would have been that Alan Crystal, the event organiser behind it, but Uncle Bert's turned them down. I heard about it because Suzalls works in Uncle Bert's head office. Anyway, they wanted experienced Yorkshire pudding makers and were offering okay money so a bunch of us signed up. There are a few, like Rosie, who were drafted in to bolster the numbers. The event covered the cost of the ingredients, and the giant pan we are making it in, and everything else, but that ... unpleasant person,' Beefy managed, just about, to curb his language, 'Brian Pumphrey ... well, you heard him. He's not going to put up the money for the fresh ingredients we need. However,' Beefy raised his hand, placing one around Albert's shoulders as he roared, 'with our new benefactor, Albert Smith, backing us, I can guarantee the man from Guinness will be blown away by the size and rise of our giant Yorkie!'

His cheer got a cheer in response, and a round of applause too. Albert looked around for Rosie but couldn't see her anywhere. The sun was setting fast outside, and she was back here at midnight, so it made sense that she would have departed already to get some sleep. There would be a babysitter involved somewhere, he couldn't imagine she was bringing Teddy back here later.

When the applause died down, Gary was waiting patiently. His stomach had begun to rumble, and a cold pint of beer sounded good; this was his weekend off after all – a proper weekend off where he wouldn't get nagged to mow the lawn or fix the tumble dryer. At least, that was what he fantasised about on the train ride up from London. He was beginning to suspect, though, that his father might yet make the weekend a little busier and more complicated than it needed to be.

Dinner

Opposite the venue, they stopped in a tavern boasting the finest steak and kidney pies in the world. It was unnecessary hyperbole, but the tactic worked, nonetheless. That they also had cask ales from local breweries helped to seal their decision.

Albert's feet, ankles, knees, hips, and shoulders were beginning to ache from all the walking and standing and trying to move faster than his body truly wanted him to go. Much like Rex, he thought it had been a strange kind of day, but not one where anything terrible had happened. He had much to think about but at least no one had died. No sooner had the thought of death popped into his head, than the question of Alan's health and what might have befallen him surfaced again.

Taking a long, slow sip of his dark, amber ale, Albert set the glass back on the table. 'What do you think might have happened to the bakers' ingredients?' he asked Gary, taking a winding route to get to the questions he wanted to discuss. 'How could the flour be filled with salt?'

Gary wanted to avoid discussing his father's conspiracy theories if at all possible, yet he could not see a way of doing that now without being rude. To appease his dad, he played along, spit-balling ideas. 'I suppose it could have been accidental at the factory.'

Albert frowned. 'Surely filling sacks of flour is an automated process and is completed in a separate area of the factory. That's if the same factory even handles salt.'

'Unless we believe the inclusion of salt to be deliberate, it must have been accidental,' Gary countered. 'It was spread throughout the flour within the sacks so could not have occurred at the venue.'

Albert thought about that for a moment before responding. His natural inclination to solve a mystery made his still-tired feet twitchy. He wanted to return to the marquee to have another look at the ingredients and maybe ask some questions, but it would have to wait until after their dinner now as he could see the waitress approaching with two steaming dishes.

Both father and son had ordered the award-winning steak and kidney pie. It was two inches high with a thick crust of flaky pastry on top and a rich, meaty filling emboldened with a red wine gravy. The pieces of beef were so well-cooked they melted on the tongue like marshmallow and the kidney portion was generous. Alongside, each had a hearty serving of creamy mashed potatoes, carrots, and peas, and a separate jug of additional gravy.

Rex's head popped up to view the delicious offerings, licking his lips in a meaningful way and trying not to slobber. 'Where's mine?' he asked his human.

Albert didn't need to understand his dog's odd noises to know what Rex was asking this time. 'I'll not be able to finish this, boy,' Albert told him. 'I'll leave a little of everything for you. How's that sound?'

Rex would have preferred a plate of his own but settled down to wait beneath the table. Above him, the humans were mostly silent as they savoured their food, pausing only briefly between forkfuls to drink their beverages.

By the time their plates were empty, Albert's licked clean by Rex, the fatigue of the day was making Albert question his desire to return to the venue to ask about the caterers. He'd already paid, so it wasn't as if he were going to get his money back. It seemed more sensible to leave it until the morning, get a good night's sleep and be fresh for what promised to be an interesting day ahead. If nothing else, the promise of private lessons in making a good Yorkshire pudding would suffice.

Declining the offer of dessert, much to Rex's disappointment, Albert chose to return to the bed and breakfast. It was still only early evening, but it was fully dark outside and the lure of a hot soak in a deep bath was greater than the pull of an unsolved mystery. Telling himself he could ponder on the elements of the case while he soaked, Albert announced his intention to retire.

Gary nodded his agreement. 'I think I shall find something to watch on the television. It will be a strange experience to be able to decide for myself what I am going to watch.'

Surprised they were leaving already, but ready for his evening bowl of kibble which was already an hour overdue, Rex got to his feet. And that was when the sound of a siren reached their ears.

Getting to their feet, the inside of the tavern began to fill with the flashing blue and white light strobing in from the dark street outside. By Albert's estimate, it was right about where the ambulance had been less than an hour ago and had stopped moving.

Father and son exchanged a glance, neither voicing their thoughts but both wondering what might have happened now to attract the police.

It was cool outside, bordering on cold, and certainly a great enough difference in temperature from inside for Albert to wish he'd brought his hat and gloves along. The police car was just along the street from them and his desire to find out why was too great for him to resist.

'You're going over there, aren't you, Dad?' asked Gary, wondering why he bothered to pose the question since he already knew the answer.

Albert exhaled slowly through his nose. 'Yes, son. Are you not curious?'

'Not really, Dad, no. I expect there has been a report of something. It's just one squad car. It could be anything. You met some of the competitors earlier; maybe there was a punch up.'

Albert couldn't argue that there had been tension between the people setting up their stalls. He didn't need to reply to Gary though, for the next second, another squad car swung into view, and behind it was a crime scene van.

'I don't think this is anything minor,' Albert commented as he set off across the street. He was going inside to find out what new fate had befallen the event.

The barriers at the edge of the field had been closed again to keep people out which might have put some people off, especially since there were cops in uniform on the pavement nearby, but Albert took a handy gravy bone from his pocket, whispered, 'Rex,' quietly to get the dog's attention, and threw it into the field.

Rex's head snapped around, tracking the rough direction the gravy bone went in the dark when his human threw it. Great! A game and a treat! As his lead came free, the old man letting it go, Rex dashed under the barrier and into the dark.

His nose led him directly to his target, but when he turned around to go back, he found his human coming across the grass after him.

'Dad, I don't think you should be in there,' warned Gary. 'The police will see you if they look this way.'

'It's okay, son,' Albert called back over his shoulder. 'I work here. So do you for that matter. Unless you plan to miss out on making a world record Yorkshire pudding.'

Gary hung his head and muttered some choice words about finding a retirement home with a lock on the door. It was all pointless though because he knew he was going to follow his dad.

Albert caught up to Rex and gathered his lead. In the back area outside of the marquees, a mix of portable generators, storage containers, and delivery vans were parked on the grass and there were dozens or maybe even hundreds of ropes pinning the marquee in place. Each represented a trip hazard in the poorly lit service area beyond the part of the venue the public were meant to see. Rex kept trying to go under the ropes, forcing Albert to tug him back. 'You need to go around them not under them,' he attempted to explain.

Rex was sort of listening, but he'd caught a scent and wanted to explore it, his nose all but switching off his hearing as the alluring smell pulled him onward. It wasn't food he could smell, although there were plenty of food smells here, it was something else, something to do with one of the injustices he'd suffered today. He wanted to follow his nose to the source and see if he was right.

Struggling along in the dark behind his father, Gary was trying to catch up so he could turn his father around. This wasn't the evening he had planned at all. A few minutes ago, the old man wanted to get back to the bed and breakfast for a bath and an early night. Now they were off playing super sleuths in the dark again. Was this how his younger brother, Randall, came to get whacked on the head?

Albert heard Gary call out his name, 'Dad!' but when he turned around to look for him, he was nowhere to be seen.

Frowning into the dark at the unexpected absence of his son, his eyes were drawn down when a bout of inventive swear words exploded upward from the grass.

'Is that you, Gary?'

Rex heard the sounds of complaint coming from his head height and caught the metallic tang of blood on the air.

'Yes, Dad. Of course it's me!' hissed Gary.

'Are you alright? Did you trip on one of the pegs?'

Rex came back past his human's legs to find Gary lying facedown on the ground. He had a cut to his head which Rex licked much as he would any other wound.

Still trying to fight his way out of the rope which was now tangled about his body, the assistance from Rex was not well received. 'Arrrgh! Get off, dog!' Gary complained.

Albert waited patiently for his son to stop swearing and get back to his feet. When he finally stood up a few seconds later, the small amount of light they had showed dark liquid coating Gary's forehead.

'You seem to have cut yourself, son.'

'You think?' Gary snapped uncharitably. 'I fell over a guy rope and hit my head on the next peg in line when I fell. This place is a deadly spider's web of lethal trip hazards and the ground is soaked because Rex created a flour bomb here earlier. What on Earth are we doing, anyway?'

Albert wriggled his lips, pondering his next move. Gary wasn't a little boy anymore, but he was still his son and he was hurt and upset. Mostly Gary was upset that his dad felt a need to investigate when he saw a mystery and people in trouble. Albert wasn't blind to that, but was he to abandon the case now so Gary could watch television? 'Let's just get you inside and get that cut looked at, shall we? Then we can see what has happened and get back to the bed and breakfast.' Albert provided his suggestion with an upbeat tone and, of course, Gary cooled his temper and agreed.

Their meandering route to avoid the police might have resulted in Gary falling and cutting his head, but they made it to the marquee and inside without being stopped or challenged.

Coming through the same door they escaped through earlier when the cloud of flour chased them from the marquee, they spotted a sight they might never forget.

Murder?

At the far end of the marquee, where the bakers had their line of oversized mixing machines, a crowd had gathered. It was formed of the bakers, more than four, so some who were not doing the night shift were yet to go home, and the police. They were all standing around the leftmost of the four giant machines, but there was no question why. Sticking up from the top of the machine was a pair of legs. It was almost cartoonish and might have been laughable were it not for the fact that the owner of the legs was not moving. That no one was rushing to get the person out could only mean they were already beyond saving, but the worst of it was that Albert recognised the legs or, more accurately, the shoes.

'Is that Brian?' asked Gary.

Remembering his son's injury, Albert swung around to look up at Gary's forehead. He had a small, but deep cut which he was holding two fingers on to stem the bleeding. Like all head wounds, it was leaking bright red blood in copious quantities.

Rather than answer Gary's question, Albert clicked his tongue at Rex, 'Go ahead, Rex, let's see what happened.'

Rex was sniffing the air but doing so tentatively because it was filled with a pungent smell of aniseed.

Moving toward the crowd at the far end of the marquee, Albert began to detect a faint smell. 'Can you smell aniseed?' he asked his son.

Gary sniffed the air. 'Yeah, kind of.'

Looking at his son, still holding his head as bright red blood ran over his fingers, he said, 'I think we should get someone to close that for you. They must have a first aid kit around here somewhere.'

Their footsteps in the otherwise quiet marquee were enough to draw the attention of the people gathered around the mixing machine. A man in a suit, one of a pair of detectives, murmured something to one of the uniformed officers. Albert guessed it was instructions to send the two men and the dog away or to corral them into a safe space so they could be questioned later, but Beefy, his head rising above that of everyone else, spotted Albert too.

'He's with us,' he announced loudly to stop the police officer from turning Albert, Gary, and Rex away. Then, ignoring the police around him, he detached himself from the crowd and came toward Albert. 'You're not going to believe what happened.' Beefy looked terrified; his face was white and for good reason since he'd threatened to do exactly what had happened just a couple of hours ago.

'That's Brian in the mixer and he's dead?' Albert hazarded.

Beefy's forehead wrinkled, 'Um, yeah,' he said, surprised. However, Albert's guess was heard by everyone, not least of which was the detectives, who turned his way.

'We just found him like that,' said one of the bakers - a man, but too far away for Albert to see who.

'And you are, sir?' asked one of the detectives, detaching himself from the group around the mixer with Brian's feet poking from it.

Reaching the front of the gathered people, Albert tugged Rex's lead to make him stop. Focussing his eyes on the detective who spoke, a man nearing fifty with a pot belly and thinning hair, Albert extended his hand.

'Albert Smith, a former detective superintendent from Kent. I'm on the team attempting the world record tomorrow. I saw the squad cars outside and thought I'd better come to investigate.' Then he made a half turn to bring Gary into the conversation. 'This is my son, Gary Smith. He's a serving detective superintendent from the Metropolitan police. He could do with a hand if someone has a first aid kit handy.'

Handshakes were exchanged, a professional courtesy on the part of the York detectives who were sergeants called Heaton and Calin. Heaton, the elder with the pot belly was a short Caucasian man reaching barely five and a half feet. His partner, Calin was Indian or perhaps Bangladeshi; Albert could not be more exact than that, but they had responded when the suspicious death was reported, arriving moments after the first squad car.

'You are familiar with the victim?' Calin asked.

Albert was by himself while Gary had his head looked at. They were standing just a few feet from the legs sticking almost straight upright out of the mixer. It was a macabre scene, yet the body needed to remain in place until evidence could be gathered.

'I met him just a few hours ago,' Albert revealed. 'I only arrived in York last night. My son got in just after lunchtime today.'

Calin had a notebook in his hand, poised to take note of what Albert might have to say, and paused to raise an eyebrow. 'How is it you come to be on the team of bakers?' he wanted to know. 'If you only arrived last night.'

Albert took a few moments to regale the detective with the story of Alan Crystal's failed mugging, the serendipitous meeting outside the museum and the events that followed.

Detective Sergeant Calin nodded along, making notes as he went. 'Mr Pumphrey was against the world record attempt?'

Albert sighed for there was an important detail he'd knowingly omitted. He was on the other side of the police investigation now and understood first-hand what it was like to want to be convenient with the truth. When he failed to respond to DS Calin's question, the detective looked up from his notebook.

Albert knew he was about to be prompted for an answer, so he told him what he should have said already. 'There was a verbal altercation a few hours ago. It involved Mr Pumphrey and most of the bakers.' Albert paused, organising the words in his head because he wanted to paint the picture correctly. DS Calin was seasoned enough to wait patiently. 'One of the bakers ... his shirt has the name Beefy written on it.'

'I know which one he is,' DS Calin assured Albert.

Albert blew out a frustrated breath. 'Mr Pumphrey tried to pull the plug on the record attempt and tempers got a little frayed.' Albert could not come up with a way to put a positive spin on what he had to say next. 'Beefy threatened to stuff Mr Pumphrey into the mixer.'

DS Calin wrote down what Albert told him word for word, then closed his notebook. 'I see. I think perhaps I ought to have a chat with Mr Botham.'

'I don't think he did it,' Albert got in quickly.

DS Calin gave him the one raised eyebrow again. 'And why is that? From what you just told me, he had motive, and opportunity.'

'He's a baker. His threat was made in the heat of the moment when he thought Mr Pumphrey was going to scupper their work. The threat was nullified.'

'By you,' DS Calin pointed out.

Albert nodded. 'Yes, by me. Beefy had no reason to harm Mr Pumphrey.'

DS Calin cut his eyes at the mixer with the feet still sticking from the top of it. 'Yet he came to harm anyway, Mr Smith. Someone stuffed him into the mixer and even though Mr Pumphrey looks to be a small man, it would take more than one person to lift him and shove him in there. Or perhaps ...' he turned his head to look at Beefy, 'just one rather large man.' Albert could not easily form an argument against the detective's logic. If their roles were reversed, he would be presenting the same argument. 'Thank you, Mr Smith,' the detective said, rising to his feet. He left Albert, caught his colleague's attention, and pointed toward Beefy who already looked nervous. The bakers were gathered a few yards away where the uniformed police had taken them. There were other people in the marquee still, some of the competitors they saw earlier had come through from their wing of the marquee to investigate the noise and fuss. Like the bakers, they were being attended to by a couple of the uniformed officers and questioned as to what they might have seen or heard.

Next to Albert, the crime scene chaps were getting ready to extricate poor Mr Pumphrey but discussing whether they ought to take the whole thing to the lab so they could preserve all the evidence. Albert wondered where the cat was, and hoped he wasn't to be found in the mixer too.

Rex had no such concerns and would happily discover the cat had been turned into a Yorkshire pudding.

With external stitches holding the wound shut, Gary came to join his father and got close enough to peer into the mixer. 'Terrible way to go,' he commented.

Albert heard his son but didn't reply. He was thinking. What he was thinking was whether the crime scene chaps would reveal a head injury on Mr Pumphrey. He walked across to the bakers, tagging onto the end away from where the detectives were talking to Beefy. The baker he came to first bore the name 'Dave 1' on his white jacket. It made Albert squint at the others where his eyes immediately found 'Dave 3'. He remembered then that there were to be three Daves on the midnight to breakfast shift. They hadn't taken themselves home yet, but would there even be a shift now? How much more of the ingredients had they lost in the batch containing Mr Pumphrey. That wasn't what he came over to ask though.

'Dave,' Albert said quietly to get the man's attention. When he turned his head, Albert asked, 'Where was everyone when Mr Pumphrey went into the mixer?' Dave gave him a blank, confused look in return. 'I assume you weren't watching.'

Dave's expression shifted to one of horror. 'God, no! What a thing to ask.'

'So where was everyone? You are here mixing up the batter to go into the machine, but somehow Mr Pumphrey ends up in mixer number one.'

'That's mixer number four, actually,' Dave pedantically corrected.

Albert ignored him. 'What I mean is - Mr Pumphrey went into the machine, but how is it that no one saw it?' Dave shrugged, so Albert persisted. 'Did you hear a scream?'

'A scream?' Dave repeated.

'Yes. Someone must have found Mr Pumphrey. Did they scream?' A hand grabbing his elbow turned out to be Gary.

'Dad, the local police can do this. There's no need for you to be involved. You know how much the police dislike it when the public interfere.'

Albert fought the wrinkle appearing on his brow. 'But I am not interfering, son. I'm wondering where everyone else was when Mr Pumphrey went into the mixer.'

'That sounds just like interfering to me, Dad. There are two detectives here. They seem perfectly capable. You were telling me how tired you were earlier. How about we call it a night? I'll make sure the local police have our contact details and know where to find us.' Gary was doing his best to be gently persuasive but with an unmistakable subtext that he would get more insistent shortly.

While the humans argued, Rex continued to sniff the air. He wanted to explore what he could smell. It was the faint, but also distinctive scent of the moped he chased earlier. You might think all automobiles smell the same, but not to a trained nose. It was a less exact science than tracking humans, but he could generally discern one vehicle from another and though he didn't know it, he was picking out each vehicle's unique blend of disgusting hydrocarbons. Tiny variations in the quantities of oil, water vapour, and the type, or even brand, of fuel used, made a difference.

'What about the ingredients?' argued Albert. 'Is there enough left to make the pudding now they have lost even more?' He switched tactic on Gary, making his enquiries about the pudding and not the apparent murder.

Gary flapped an arm into the air in a motion of exasperation. His father was such a determined old codger when he wanted to be. He was in half a mind to abandon the old fool to his daft private sleuthing so he could head to a pub and then get to bed. If they were now short on ingredients, would they abandon the attempt or was his father about to stump up more money? Could it even go ahead now that they had a probable murder at the venue?

Picking up Albert's question, Dave 1 answered, 'I think it is just the one batch we lost. We need one thousand of them to have enough for the record attempt. I know Beefy ordered some extra as a contingency.'

Gary had been briefly hoping the record attempt wouldn't be able to proceed and he would get his day back. That hope, too, was rudely snatched away.

'At least, I think so,' said Dave 1.

Albert slapped a hand on Dave 1's shoulder. 'Maybe we should go and check,' he suggested.

Dave 1 looked a little startled, but said, 'Oh, err, yeah, maybe someone should. We keep losing time, and it looks like we are going to lose mixer four. I don't think we would use it even if they did take Mr Pumphrey out and leave it behind.'

They clearly were not going to do that because the crime scene guys were already walking it toward the door, employing a couple of spare uniformed cops to help keep it steady.

As Dave 1 and Albert started to move, heading for the storeroom outside, one of the officers keeping the bakers in a group asked, 'Where are you going?'

Albert fielded the question. 'Just going to the gents,' he revealed with an embarrassed smile. 'Can't hold it the way I used to be able to.'

The cop couldn't come up with an argument to stop the old man; he didn't want to deal with some old codger having an incontinence issue. However, he did point at Dave 1. 'Why's he going?'

'He's my helper,' Albert lied ambiguously, basically daring the young police officer to ask which part of the task he required help with.

The cop had no desire to find out. 'Yeah, okay. Come straight back, please.' He joined to chase criminals and be a hero, not worry about old men and their dodgy bladders.

'I think I'll just wait here,' said Gary, looking about to see if there was somewhere he could sit. When his father returned, he was going to insist they leave. The local detectives wouldn't resist his request to leave the scene and it looked like they were about to arrest Beefy anyway.

Outside, they crossed the soggy grass toward a pair of shipping containers. They were both closed but not locked. Dave 1, away from the ears of the police, decided to get chatty. 'I think most of us were out here when the shout came. It was Beefy who found him. He sent us out to get a fresh pallet of ingredients for the next few batches of batter. You might think it would ruin being made up so far in advance of baking it, but the batter works better, and rises farther, when it has been left to rest for a few hours.'

Albert learned something, for he had never made the batter in advance when trying to make the pudding at home for himself. Had that been Petunia's secret too?

'Best leave the dog outside,' said Dave 1. 'It's all very well having the dog in the marquee where we can separate him from the food preparation area, but we shouldn't let him go in here with the ingredients.'

Albert looked around for something to hook his lead on to, but they were in a field. He would have to traipse back to the marquee or fifty yards to a van to find something he could fix Rex to. Accepting defeat, he held the end of the lead in front of Rex's mouth. 'Can you hold this, Rex?'

Rex, surprised by the request, felt his eyebrows rise, but obediently opened his mouth. What was his human up to?

Trusting that they would only be inside for a few seconds, Albert said, 'Stay, Rex,' while Dave 1 wrestled the right hand door open, then followed him inside. The container had light and power and was refrigerated to maintain the dairy products stored within.

None of that was of particular interest to Rex. The moment his human was no longer in sight, he turned around and started following his nose. He wanted to find the moped. His human would probably be displeased that Rex wasn't outside when he next looked, but Rex was choosing to exploit a small loophole in the command 'stay' because his human hadn't been specific about where he should stay.

That it was dark had no effect on Rex's sense of smell. If anything, the reduction of human activity in darkness made it easier to sort and follow scents. It still confused him that humans, like his human's pup, could fall over in the dark, but he knew they refused to use their strongest sense, foolishly trusting their eyes despite claiming it was too dark to see.

With his eyes closed and his nose in the air, he located a direction for the moped scent and began a loping canter to get to it.

Inside the container, Albert was helping Dave 1 to count the eggs. This was the refrigerated container Dave 1 had explained. It housed the milk, eggs, oil, and salt. The last two ingredients didn't need to be kept chilled, but there was no room in the second container which was full to the brim with flour. The eggs were in caterers' packs of hundreds, stacked one atop the other. Dave crouched right down to make sure the bottom boxes were both full and intact and was about to get up when he stiffened. Albert saw it, wondering whether the man had seen a large spider and was about to scream.

Instead, Dave 1 reached out with his left hand to pluck something from the floor. It was a button, Albert saw. 'What have you got there?'

Dave 1 stood up with the button resting in his palm. 'Just a button,' he said. It wasn't just a button though; it was a very ornate button with a three-dimensional cameo face of a woman on it. Such a thing wasn't what you found on an everyday item of clothing, and it was large – more than half an inch across, so it was also not the sort of button one might find on a man's shirt either.

Albert stared at it. 'Could it have come from someone's coat?' he asked.

Dave 1 turned it over, his expression curious. 'No. No one has buttons on their baking clothes, and no one would come in here in their normal clothes.'

A voice from the entrance startled them both. 'Gentlemen, I thought you were going to the restroom.'

Albert, his heart pumping madly for a couple of beats, saw the face framed in the doorway was the young police officer he lied to about his destination. He compounded his earlier lie with another. 'We decided to check on the supplies. With Mr Pumphrey encased in a load of batter, we were worried whether we would still have enough for the record attempt.'

The police officer either wasn't bothering to listen or had no interest in what Albert was saying. 'Are you done?' he demanded to know in a bored tone.

Albert stepped in front of Dave 1, plucking the button from his palm, and pocketing it. 'Yes, officer, quite done. Thank you.'

Dave 1 shot the old man an enquiring look from the side of his face but didn't say anything in front of the officer. Was a button evidence? Maybe. Albert figured he wouldn't know until he found where it had come from. He already had a good guess lined up, but no idea when he might get to test it.

Coming out of the container, the officer paused, and with a frown, asked, 'Didn't you have a dog?'

Rex's nose led him onwards, but he was beginning to doubt that he was tracking the scent of the moped. There was something wrong about it … something human. It was the same scent, yet different.

When the answer came to him, it was like a gut punch – he was smelling the moped on a human! Was it the one he chased earlier today, the one who cheated in their game of chase and bite? It could be, Rex knew, but he couldn't be certain because he had been too busy chasing to get a good grasp of the human's scent.

If he assumed it was the same human, then he was here now, in the same location as the human in the suit he was trying to hurt in the alleyway. Was he here earlier when Rex had been chasing the cat? The disappointing answer to that question was probably a yes and he'd been too distracted to notice.

The sound of his human's voice reached his ears, pricking them up, but as Rex turned to go, he caught something on the wind.

Blood.

Turning his whole body toward the breeze, Rex closed off his other senses and tried to catch it again.

'Rex!'

Rex heard the shout but filtered it out. If he could hear his human shouting, then his human was okay, and he could go to him shortly. Right now, he needed to focus on finding the source of the blood. It was on the wind, and like the moped's exhaust scent, it was almost intangible. Almost but not quite.

When he caught it again, he set off, running quickly but not sprinting. There was blood on the air, and it was human. It usually was in Rex's experience. He was forced to weave through the storage containers, trucks, vans, and cars again, but his nose led him on, and he could see just fine in the dark. Coming through the last line of vehicles, now well away from the marquee, he saw a human.

The human, a male, was framed in the dim moonlight peering through the clouds above, but now the smell of blood was dominating Rex's olfactory system and he was having trouble picking up what the man smelled of.

Then he realised, the man also smelled of blood, but it wasn't his, he was just covered in enough of it to mask his natural odour. The source of the blood was a lump lying on the ground twenty yards behind the human bathed in moonlight.

Rex barked, which he realised afterward was the wrong thing to do. The human broke into a sprint; walking one moment, running as fast as he could the next. Well there was a simple decision: It was chase and bite time. His record for the day was two for nothing, and it was time to improve his batting average.

Rex's powerful back legs bunched and drove off the grass, his short claws digging in to give him purchase. This far away from the marquee, the ground hadn't been saturated by the water washing the flour away. It was what racehorses might call good to firm and was perfect for sprinting on.

The injured human lying on the grass needed help, Rex felt certain of that. The scent of blood was strong enough that there had to be a lot of it. However, helping the human would require more humans so Rex concentrated on the thing he knew how to do: chase the criminal.

Almost back at the marquee, Albert heard Rex bark once. It came from way over in the other side of the field. 'What is that dog up to now?' he muttered, wishing he hadn't trusted Rex to hold his own lead. He needed to find Gary and go after Rex. His son was right that it was bedtime but retiring would now have to wait until he found Rex again.

Glancing to his right, he saw Beefy Botham being taken away. The detectives had arrested him, and Albert couldn't blame them for that. Beefy insisted he was innocent but admitted he sent everyone away to get ingredients and was in the marquee by himself. He then refused to account for how he hadn't seen Brian and didn't know how he could have ended up in the mixer. Albert knew he would have arrested him too - the death threat earlier was really damning, especially since that was exactly how Brian came to die.

The police were wrapping up; they had statements, and a suspect in custody, the crime scene guys had a body to process - once they got him out of the batter – so they were about done too.

That was until they heard the dog start to howl mournfully.

Does Anyone Speak Dog?

Rex chased the human across the grass. Whoever it was had a big lead and Rex had to run up an incline to get to him, but even so, Rex did not expect to be beaten for the third time on the same day. He was fast enough to close the distance, but he couldn't see what was ahead in the dead ground.

Powering onward, closing the gap between them with each bound, he needed just a few more strides to bring down his quarry. Thoughts of whether the human carried a weapon flashed through his mind but were dismissed: his job was to bring the criminal down, and even though no command to do so had been given, he knew it was the right thing to do.

Ten yards apart, then five, then defying logic, the human vanished.

Rex was trusting his eyes for the chase, he didn't need his nose to catch the human, but he was there one moment and not the next. Two strides later, Rex saw why and had to throw on the brakes to try to stop himself. The field ended at the river. The smell of the river was all around, fading into the background the way paint on a wall does when there are things on the wall to look at.

Panicking as he questioned whether he could possibly stop in time, Rex cursed himself for not detecting how strong the river now smelled. Digging his claws in, he managed to swing his body around so he was at least sliding backwards; it gave him greater purchase with his claws and that made the difference between going over and stopping in time. As it was, his back end went over the edge and he had to scrape his claws against the stonework to get back onto the grass.

Looking down, he could see the human descending a long ladder set into the stone. He was already twenty feet below Rex and moving as fast as his hands and feet would allow. Rex paced, barking into the darkness though he knew it would do no good: the human had escaped.

He couldn't get down, and if there were a way around to reach the riverside below safely, the human would be long gone by the time he got there. Any hopes that he might be able to track the scent was instantly doused when the man reached the bottom rung, ran across the jetty, and dove into the river.

That the human escaped, and it was three games of chase and bite lost in a single day, wasn't what made him howl though. Since he couldn't catch the criminal, his next task was to check the victim. Rex didn't know who it was – the scent of the human was too deeply masked by the tang of blood for Rex to make out anything else - but the sound of rasping breaths along with the stench of blood leaking into the grass told him the human needed help of a kind a dog couldn't administer.

He needed to get the attention of the humans, but if he ran back to where they were, they might try to clip him onto his lead. When he got close enough, the victim spotted him. Moving his head slightly, the human tried to speak, creating nothing but a rasping noise. One weak arm lifted in Rex's direction, making the dog feel inadequate for possibly the first time in his life.

Beginning to panic for the human, he tipped back his head and howled.

It was less than a minute later when the police spotted him. Rex heard them shouting his name, heard them getting closer, and when he saw them jogging uncertainly as they came around the line of containers and trucks, he started barking.

He was sitting by the human so could tell that he was still alive, but also that he wasn't doing very well. He danced back as the humans advanced, making sure they could see the stricken victim on the ground.

Someone said, 'Good dog,' but the focus was all about the injured human. The humans were calling for help and one of them was using his radio - not that Rex could understand that – to call for medical emergency services.

Rex sat on his haunches and watched, panting lightly still from the effort of the chase. Presently, he spotted his human coming up the incline toward him. His tail started wagging all by itself, happiness propelling it back and forth.

Albert spotted Rex easily when he came around the side of the trucks and into the open. Rex was silhouetted against the night sky, his proud outline a black shape with the stars behind him. Albert couldn't yet be sure what the dog had found, but Albert's worry that Rex might be hurt dissipated now that he could see him. The police officers were all focused on something to Rex's right; Albert could see three or maybe four kneeling on the ground. They were shouting instructions and it sounded like they were talking to someone who was hurt or injured in some way.

Gary asked, 'You see him, Dad? Rex is all right.' He was relieved for his father, but also for himself because he knew the pain of losing a pet. With his mother gone, Rex was the focus of his father's life.

Albert called out, 'Rex, come!' and was doubly relieved to see the dog sprinting effortlessly. He wasn't injured or hurt, he was just fine, and he'd done himself proud, finding an injured person and alerting people so they could help him.

'There was a human,' Rex said. 'He ran away and climbed down the ladder. Then he went for a swim.'

Gary stared down at the dog who was hopping from paw to paw and spinning on the spot. Albert was trying to get hold of the lead which still hung loose from Rex's collar, but the dog wouldn't stay still long enough.

97

As one of the officers came running back down the slope, Gary asked, 'What have you got?'

The officer didn't slow his pace, but he knew the man who asked the question was a serving senior officer, so he replied, 'A stabbing, sir. A nasty one. I'm not sure he will make it.' He was gone before he could say anything further, most likely heading to the road to guide in the paramedics.

Albert blew out a huff of breath and turned to face his son. 'Still think there's nothing going on here?'

Gary grimaced in the dark: he hated to admit that his father might have a point. 'This could be completely unrelated, Dad.'

Rex was getting impatient with being ignored. 'Hey!' he barked, jolting his human to make him listen and darting back up the slope to show them where the attacker had gone.

'Is he all right?' asked Gary, wondering if the dog had a screw loose.

Albert started to follow the dog. 'He's trying to tell me something.'

Gary didn't move. 'It's a dog,' he pointed out.

Albert didn't argue with his son's factually correct observation, but said, 'Yes. He's a dog who is trying to tell me something.'

Rex saw his human walking the direction he wanted him to go and shot off up the slight incline. The police officers were still tending to the injured human he found, but he couldn't be any help there anyway. What he could do, was get someone to listen to what he had to tell them about the human he chased.

'He ran this way and he went into the river,' Rex tried to explain.

Remembering the torch on his phone, Albert dug around in his pocket to produce it and then fumbled around until he got it working. Rex, by then, was standing at the edge and looking over at the ladder. Albert joined him, cautiously looking over and down. 'What are you trying to tell me, boy? Did you chase someone?'

Rex spun on the spot and barked.

Albert skewed his lips to one side in thought. 'That was a yes, wasn't it, Rex?'

Again, Rex did his excited dance. Left behind at the bottom of the incline, Gary had muttered and moaned at himself until he caught himself doing it, and worrying that he was sounding petulant and petty, he struck off to follow his old dad.

'Have you found something?' he asked once he was close enough for his father to hear without needing to raise his voice.

Albert wondered how to answer. 'I think Rex chased someone. There are boot marks here.'

'Then we are trampling all over the crime scene, Dad, and should move away.'

Albert wasn't about to move even though he knew Gary was right. 'No one would know there was a crime scene if it were not for Rex.' He pointed to the ladder which Gary was yet to come close enough to see. 'Whoever it was got away by climbing down a ladder. Rex couldn't follow, but he knew well enough to alert us all to the victim. Do they know who he is?'

'The victim?' Gary clarified. 'I haven't asked, Dad. Look, you might be right and there is something happening here, but it's still their beat, not mine. If I had a copper from York in my neck of the woods, I would politely insist he tell me what he knows and then go promptly away. I am not going to be that policeman who is a policeman everywhere he goes.'

His son's response surprised him, but maybe things were different now than they had been in his day. He collected Rex's lead finally, the dog no longer moving around each time he tried to grab it. He was about to say something, but the collective noises from the police officers tending to the injured man told him the victim had just lost his battle.

A heartbeat later, the young officer who ran off to get the paramedics returned, running all the way. The paramedics were with him, lugging their heavy bags, and though they attempted to revive the man, Albert could see from their body language that they knew they were fighting a losing battle.

The two detectives, Calin and Heaton were watching, staying with the action there until it played out. They would have wanted to have the man identify his attacker and had most likely been impatiently waiting for the paramedics to arrive and stabilise him. Too late now, their questions would go unanswered.

Albert chose to go to them. 'I think my dog chased the attacker away. There are footprints at the top of the rise, and you might be able to get a set of fingerprints. There's a ladder leading down to the river's edge.'

Calin sounded surprised when he said, 'Thank you, Mr Smith. That's helpful of you.'

'That's two murders in a single evening,' murmured Heaton. 'I'm calling the crime scene guys back.'

He took his phone from a trouser pocket, but before he could make the call Albert pointed out, 'You don't know Mr Pumphrey was murdered.'

'Dad,' warned Gary.

'He could have slipped,' Albert argued though he knew it sounded weak.

DS Heaton paused with his phone in his hand. 'You think he climbed on the mixer and got inside it while it was running? What would possess him to be anywhere near it? He wasn't involved in the baking so far as I am aware. In fact, I believe Mr Botham murdered Mr Pumphrey because he was so set against the baking.' He said it dismissively and turned away to make his call without waiting to hear what Albert might say next.

Albert wasn't about to say anything though; he'd just glimpsed a possibility and now he needed to check something out.

DS Calin watched his partner step away but let him go. Facing the old man and his detective superintendent son once more, he said, 'Mr Botham has already been taken to the station. We were just about to go ourselves when your dog started howling. So, of course, you realise, if we are right about Mr Botham killing Mr Pumphrey, there is a second killer at this contest.'

It was last orders when they finally made it to a pub. So much of their afternoon and evening had been absorbed in dealing with paramedics, the fire brigade, or the police, that to Gary, it felt like a harder than normal day at work. He was tired, and only stopped for a drink before bed because his father suggested it.

'I think Rex deserves a half pint of stout and a packet of crisps,' Albert declared. Rex looked up at his human approvingly and got a pat on his head and scratch behind his ears as added reward while they waited for the bar lady to serve them. Albert ordered a gin and tonic and a pint of lager for Gary, then sagged into a chair at a table near the door.

From his backpack, the trusty metal dog bowl appeared once more. He gave Rex the crisps first, bacon flavour because he was convinced that is what a dog would pick. Eight seconds later when the crisps were gone, he poured the stout into the now empty bowl and ruffled Rex's fur while the dog lapped away at the black liquid.

Before they left the competition venue, there had been much discussion about what might now happen to the event. Two separate, and potentially unrelated murders, were still two murders. Albert's argument that Mr Pumphrey might have slipped into the mixer by himself was given no credence, not even by Gary. The deaths happened within an hour of one another, making the venue or the event appear to be the catalyst. Was there something about the Yorkshire pudding competition that was driving people crazy?

Albert noted the detectives either were not aware or had not yet made the connection with the earlier incident that saw Alan Crystal hospitalised. His bout of terrible vomiting could, yet again, be completely unrelated. It most likely was, but what if it wasn't? Calin and Heaton had not factored it in, and they appeared unconcerned about the ingredient tampering which might have been a factor in Brian Pumphrey's death.

Their boss arrived shortly after the second man was pronounced dead at the scene, and it was his arrival that sparked the discussion about the event. In the marquee, the poor bakers, still reeling from the arrest of Beefy and the possibility that he had chosen to kill the show's organiser, were trying to continue with the preparation for the giant pudding. There were thousands of people due to arrive in the morning: competitors, visitors, vendors, and happy shoppers, plus the man from Guinness.

Chief Inspector Doyle, a thin, balding, morose man in his late forties, wanted to shut the event and declare the whole thing a crime scene.

'If you do that, the killer will be gone,' argued Albert at the time. He and Gary were not involved in the conversation, they were standing a few feet away where Albert was close enough to overhear what the policemen were saying. His comment elicited an explanation from the two detectives about who the old man, his dog, and son were.

Turning his attention their way, CI Doyle asked, 'Why will the killer be gone? Isn't he already gone?'

Albert figured he had one shot at this, an exhaled breath ruffling his cheeks as he stepped forward to explain his thoughts. 'You suspect there is more than one killer?' he sought to have them clarify out loud.

DS Heaton fielded the question with a bored tone, 'There has to be. We took Botham into custody twenty minutes before the second victim was stabbed.'

As kindly as he could, Albert said, 'You are assuming Botham killed Mr Pumphrey.'

His response caused Heaton's eyes to flare, so too those of DS Calin, but CI Doyle was interested in what Albert had to say. 'I thought Botham was a good fit?' he accused his two sergeants.

'He is,' argued Calin. 'He threatened to kill the man in public in the exact way the victim then met his end. He also made sure he was alone in the marquee by sending the rest of his bakers away. He is the one member of that team who cannot account for his whereabouts and he is the one who found the body.'

Albert didn't need to be reminded that the one who last saw a victim alive is usually the killer. Beefy would have to come up with an explanation for his whereabouts when the death occurred if he wanted to prove his innocence. What he said was, 'Regardless, he denied the murder.' As all eyes swung his way, he followed his comment up with, 'Consider this: Botham could not have killed both victims, but the second victim's killer could have. What you have is two deaths without clear reason, but the likelihood they are both something to do with the event being held here tomorrow.'

The chief inspector was frowning deeply at the old man. 'Which is precisely the reason why the event should be cancelled. It's not like it is a major mark in the calendar, it's just some daft competition to bake a giant Yorkshire pudding.'

Albert shook his head. 'If I may be so bold, I feel you are missing the point.' The chief inspector's brow furrowed deeper yet, but he didn't interrupt Albert when he said, 'For the people involved, the event and the competition is important enough to kill for. Are you aware the prize for the best Yorkshire pudding is a contract to supply the high-end supermarket chain Bentley Brothers?'

The chief inspector's expression betrayed his lack of knowledge on the subject. 'I don't see what that has to do with ...'

'The winner will have their recipe for Yorkshire puddings in every Bentley Brothers store. There is also a ten-thousand-pound prize for winning, the money for which has been put up by Ethan Bentley himself, but the chance to supply Bentley Brothers for the foreseeable future is worth how much?'

No one knew the answer, but their exchanged glances all said the same thing: however much it was worth, it was a lot. Ethan Bentley was well known for being the lead entrepreneur on the television show *Brilliant Business Ideas*, where undiscovered inventors and unsuccessful entrepreneurs offered their brilliant business ideas to a panel of multi-millionaires. Most of the people coming on the show were sent away empty handed, but those who impressed the panel often went on to become millionaires themselves.

Albert summed up what they were all thinking. 'It's enough to want to kill for. If you close the event, the killer will vanish. If you assume the money is the motivator behind at least the second death, then tomorrow the killer will be here trying to win it.'

'Or threatening yet more lives,' countered Detective Sergeant Heaton. 'If you are right,' he hit the word 'if' hard to make a point, 'then you are inviting the shark back to prey on more unsuspecting bathers.'

The chief inspector was the one who would have to make the decision and Albert knew it was a tough one so stayed quiet and hoped while he watched the man's face. On one hand, Albert knew he was right about the killer vanishing if the event was forced to cancel by the police. They could do it easily by just declaring the venue a crime scene. Politically, it was shaky ground, but if he didn't close it and someone else died ...'

When he looked up, his eyes were on Albert. 'Your name again, sir?'

'Albert Smith.'

The chief inspector was nodding his head, reaching a decision. To Heaton and Calin, he said, 'Get back to the station and interview your suspect. If Botham is

guilty, I want a confession, it may change the scope of our investigation. If he won't confess, you need to be certain in your conviction that he did it.' The detectives had their orders and the burden of proving their suspect was involved fell to them now. Swivelling his whole body to face back toward Albert and Gary, the chief inspector nodded his head in their direction. It wasn't two civilians he was talking to, one of them was a serving senior officer, who could at any time, if he so chose, pull rank and be a pain. That he hadn't done so demanded respect. 'Thank you for your help this evening, gentlemen. Most especially you, sir,' he dipped his head directly at Gary. 'I have to ask that you vacate the area now so my team can do what is necessary. Tomorrow, I will have officers working in plain clothes at the event. My understanding is that you will both be there?'

'That's correct,' replied Gary, trying not to sound upset about it.

The chief inspector pursed his lips in a moment of thought. 'I will tell them to identify themselves to you. You clearly have keen eyes for trouble, but I must ask that if you spot anything, you inform my officers.' He focussed his eyes on Gary. 'I'm sure you understand, sir, how much easier it will be if the local officers make the arrests.'

Gary raised a hand in submission. 'Have no fear, Chief Inspector, I never planned to get involved in the first place.'

That was half an hour ago now, Gary insisting they left the venue immediately after they concluded the business with the chief inspector so they stood the slim chance of making it back to the bar for last orders. His fantasy of a night hogging the television remote was gone, so too his father's plans for a bath.

'How are you feeling, Dad?' Gary asked as he placed his almost empty pint glass back on the table.

Albert went for the honest answer. 'A little fatigued, son. I should have quit hours ago.' It would be easy to slip into a cycle of moaning about the various parts of him that either ached or didn't work the same way they used to. Instead, he shot his eldest child a grin and flipped his eyebrows. 'It's nothing a few hours' sleep and a good breakfast won't sort out in the morning.'

Gary picked up his pint again hoping that might be true.

Squirrels

Rex awoke to the sound of something outside the window. It sounded suspiciously like squirrels, a menace which had blighted his life for as long as he could remember. The need to chase the twitchy, fluffy little blighters was hardwired into his DNA at such a base level, he never once thought to question it.

They needed to be stopped, that was what he knew.

His human was still asleep though the first tendrils of dawn were piercing the gloom outside. Rex couldn't tell what time it was, but it felt like an appropriate time for him to be allowed out for a walk – he had business to attend to. Breakfast was high on his agenda too.

Normally, all it took to wake his human was sitting next to the bed and breathing in his face. Occasionally, it was necessary to give his face a lick, but the old man always seemed to disapprove of that strategy and would then be grumpy for an hour or more.

Before Rex could do either, the noise from outside the window came again, this time making him want to investigate it.

The thick curtains were drawn to keep the light out, but Rex ducked his head under and then up the other side to look out. It took three attempts because the hem of the curtain, which were floor length, kept covering his eyes. Finally able to see outside, it was lighter than he expected, which meant they had slept in longer than intended. That was secondary behind the squirrel now watching him through the window with an acorn in his paws.

Rex bared his teeth.

The squirrel twitched his tail, which Rex took to be a taunt. His paws twitched on the carpet; he wanted to get to the squirrel. It was in a tree, a large oak with thick branches, one of which ran perpendicular to the window, stopping just a foot or so shy where it had been lopped off.

Rex growled, 'I'm going to get you, squirrel.'

The squirrel, unable to translate or even hear what the dog was saying had little interest – his acorn was all consuming. Wondering what the first one was looking at; another came to join him. Then another. Soon Rex had half a dozen squirrels looking through the window at him.

Albert awoke with a start, a sudden noise ripping him from a dream about a giant platter of roast beef he needed to eat to stop his boat made of Yorkshire pudding from sinking. That the strange dream evaporated was a blessing, but fear of the unknown gripped him as the loud noise rang out again.

This time, his eyes were open, and they were drawn to the source of the noise. 'Rex!'

Startled by his human's voice, Rex spun about on the spot. Or, at least, he tried to. Getting agitated and dancing around as the squirrels taunted him with their twitchy tails, he was now standing on the right-most of the curtains. Spinning his hefty body around to look at his human resulted in the curtain going tight. Pinned as it was now at both top and bottom, it created a barrier which Rex was fighting to go through. In his head, it just needed a little more force applied.

Albert, confused and disorientated, couldn't quite work out what he was seeing. The curtains were moving about, and something looked to be trying to ram its way through one of them. In the darkness, with brief flashes of light coming around the curtain as it twitched, he heard the first ripping noise before he was able to add together the clues.

His shout of, 'Rex, no!' came at the exact moment Rex thrust off with his back legs. With his front legs pinning the curtain down, and his head barrelling forward, something had to give. With a rending sound of rawl plugs being yanked out of brick, the curtain pole above his head flew free of the wall.

Rex was momentarily triumphant as the pressure holding him back evaporated, but the heavy, lined curtain, complete with its pole, then dropped onto him, entombing him in more material than he could fight his way out of.

Muttering and swearing, with his cotton pyjamas skewwhiff, Albert flung himself out of bed to tackle the dog before he could do any more damage. 'Rex, just hold on, boy. I'll get you out. Just stop fighting!'

Getting down to the carpet to extricate the dog, who would not stop struggling and was beginning to panic inside his polyester coffin, Albert found himself swearing again when a knock came at his door.

'Everything all right in there, Dad?'

'Not exactly,' he called back. Now that he was on the carpet, not the simplest process at his age, he had to get back up again. His back protested from the too-early-in-the-day demands placed upon it and his knees clicked multiple times as if being wound against a ratchet. The bundle of curtain continued to spasm and jerked as Rex fought for freedom, but Albert went for the door first, letting Gary in so he could help.

Gary was wearing sports gear and was covered in a sheen of sweat: he'd been out for a run. He had a set of wireless headphones sticking out of his ears, the right-most of which he'd popped out to be able to hear better.

Albert's room was still gloomy because the day outside was still getting started, but there was enough light to see the curtain pole hanging from one mount and the dog bucking like a bronco under a swathe of material.

Gary's eyes went wide at the sight, his father stepping out of the way to let him come in. 'If you please, son.'

Gary said, 'Righto,' popping out his other earbud and placing both it and his phone on Albert's bed. On his knees, Gary had Rex freed from his blanket of terror in seconds.

Rex popped out and spun around to see if the squirrels were still watching, trampling on the fallen curtain again to get back to them as they watched through the window with mild curiosity. Behind him the humans were wafting the air.

'Wow!' gasped Gary. 'I guess he got a little panicked under the curtain and let something go. That is making my eyes water.' Before Albert could do anything to stop him, Gary grabbed the catch for the sash window. 'I'll just let that air out for a moment.' He threw the window upwards and open, causing the squirrels to scatter.

A younger version of Albert might have thrown himself forward into a dive to stop his dog whose back legs were already quivering as the muscles started to engage. He knew Rex was going to go, but he just couldn't get there in time to stop him

Rex's eyes were as wide as saucers! He'd never been this close to a squirrel. They were right there, darting along the thick branch a few feet in front of his nose. Something at the back of his head was telling him this was a bad idea, but he couldn't help himself. As the squirrels scarpered, his legs drove him off the carpet and out through the open window.

Only when he sailed out into free air did he remember that the squirrels were in a tree thirty feet off the ground. His front paws landed on the branch, which was far narrower than his brain had been telling him and as his back feet landed behind him, he felt true fear for the first time in his life.

The squirrels were gone; he was never going to catch them he realised as terror gripped his whole body. Paralysed now, and balancing precariously on a branch, he could hear his human behind him.

Albert was just about as dumbfounded as he had ever been in his life. He'd watched as Gary swiped his hands to grab Rex's tail and missed and then would swear his heart stopped bothering to beat until the dog landed safely on the branch. Now he had to get him back inside the building.

'Rex just back up a bit,' Albert tried. He was only about four feet from the window; if they could get hold of him, they could probably get him back. It was the probably bit that had him worried.

'What does he weigh?' asked Gary, wondering if he could go out onto the branch and pick Rex up.

Albert snorted. 'A lot.' It wasn't an accurate description, but it painted the picture correctly. 'Nearly as much as me, I reckon.' Sighing, he reached for his phone.

Gary squinted at his dad. 'Who are you calling? International Rescue?'

Albert doubted even the *Thunderbirds* would be much help with this problem. And so it was that ten minutes later, wearing a coat over his pyjamas and a pair of shoes on his bare feet, he came to be standing outside Mrs Morton's bed and breakfast waiting for the fire brigade to arrive.

Gary had taken the precaution of wrestling the mattress from his bed to place on the ground beneath Rex just in case. The landlady would most likely pitch a fit when she saw it, but he could afford to buy a new mattress. It was better than dealing with the dog falling and hurting himself and would be cheaper too.

With Gary at the rear of the building with the mattress watching Rex, Albert was left to stand in the street to welcome the firefighters. Wouldn't you know it? It was the same team again, Station Officer Hamilton gawping through the window of the fire truck as he recognised the old man.

Albert scratched his head and stared at the fallen leaves blowing about on the breeze, idly waiting until the fire truck came to a stop. Station Officer Hamilton didn't wait though, he wound down his window to shout a, 'Good morning, sir. When dispatch said there was a dog stuck in a tree, I thought it was a wind up.'

Albert met his eyes. 'I wish it were.'

Looking panicked, Mrs Morton ran out of her front door. 'Am I on fire,' she gasped, dashing into the street to look back at her building.

Albert said, 'No, Mrs Morton. My dog had a minor … error of judgement this morning. He's in the oak tree around the back.'

The landlady gawped open-mouthed as if waiting for Albert to deliver his punchline, but as the firefighters began taking long ladders from the top of their truck, she accepted that it wasn't a joke.

'This I've got to see,' she said, pulling her cardigan tight around her body against the cold to follow the procession heading for the rear of her building. They skirted the bed and breakfast, making their way along the side to the rear where they found Gary, still in his sweaty sports gear, but now looking rather chilly. Above his head, a large German Shepherd dog balanced on a branch.

'The squirrels are trying to make him fall, I think,' Gary told them with a look of disbelief on his face. 'They've been throwing acorns at him. They're not bad shots either.'

Everyone cast their eyes into the tree just in time to see an acorn bounce off Rex's skull. The dog looked utterly miserable and his legs were visibly shaking with fear.

Station Officer Hamilton clapped Albert on the shoulder. 'This is a first for me, sir. Well done.'

Albert knew he was being ribbed, but all he felt was relief that there was someone here to deal with it.

It took six firefighters, three ladders, a block and tackle and a jury-rigged safety harness to get the giant dog out of the tree and back to land.

Rex felt like licking the grass just to make sure it was real when his paws finally touched it. All the while he'd been in the tree, he'd been pondering his purpose in life and questioning whether perhaps he ought to let squirrels have their way and call it even. Now he was back on land, and out of the tree, his determination to get the fluffy horrors quadrupled.

The firefighters began to pack their gear away, Station Officer Hamilton still smiling jovially at the way his shift had started. For Gary, Albert, and Rex, it was time to get inside. Albert wanted to use the bathroom and get some breakfast. They were supposed to be at the venue already, though he knew not what might await them this morning. Had the bakers worked through the night? Were they being successful? Or had they encountered fresh problems?

Just as they started back toward the front of the building and the warmth it offered, Mrs Morton said, 'Here, is that my mattress?'

Albert felt it necessary to hurry breakfast, which was disappointing because he considered it the most important meal of the day and also, quite often, his favourite. To be fair, the part he hurried was getting dressed and feeding Rex. Rex wasn't getting a chunk of sausage off the side of his plate this morning, that was for sure.

His full-English platter of thick bacon chops, sausages, black pudding, fried bread, mushrooms, eggs, and grilled tomato got the savouring it deserved, but he skipped his second cup of tea in favour of getting to the museum for the competition. He had money invested in the outcome of the world record attempt now, after all.

Of course, the giant Yorkshire pudding was nothing but background noise against the bigger picture of the two deaths yesterday. Last night, he had wanted to find out about Alan Crystal's condition, but Brian Pumphrey's death and then the stabbing, and subsequent death of a definite murder victim had eaten up too much of their evening to make any further investigation tenable.

Gary had been good enough to make some enquiries using his contacts – easy when you are a serving senior officer – so they knew the identity of the murdered man. His name was Jordan Banks, a twenty-eight-year-old man from Wetherby, a town due east of York on the A1(M) motorway. The police were able to lift a set of prints from the ladder, which revealed a misdemeanour record for shoplifting that was a decade old. There was nothing since. He was employed in Wetherby in a fast food franchise and had no link to the Yorkshire pudding competition, to anyone in the competition or appearing at the event, and no link to the museum, Alan Crystal, or anyone else. No one could provide any reason for him to be in York, let alone at the venue.

Why or how Jordan Banks came to be in the field behind the marquee was yet to be determined. Equally, the motive for his murder remained unknown. Gary had a picture of the man on his phone, but he was not someone Albert recognised despite hoping he might have seen him at some point the previous day.

Arriving at the venue, they found the museum entrance open and a crowd queuing to get in. 'Perhaps we should have gone around the side again,' commented Gary, wondering how long it would take them to get inside.

As it turned out, the queue moved swiftly, taking them up to the ticket booth where they flashed their VIP lanyards again. Inside the booth was the same man as yesterday, looking just as bored as before as he handed out tickets and took the visitors' money. Albert and Gary got a nod as they went by, the man's attention already on the next person in line.

Alan's idea that the museum might attract a lot more interest was proving to be true as the corridors and rooms they passed were packed with people reading the information on the walls and looking at the pictures and exhibits as they transitioned through the old house to the marquee at the back. Big signs were hung everywhere to ensure no one would have any trouble finding their way to the competition, but Albert made his way through all of it, remembering the route from yesterday.

Caused to pause briefly by a bottleneck of people ahead to them, Albert turned his head to look at a picture on the wall beside him when it caught his eye. 'Look, Gary,' he drew his son's attention with a nudged elbow. 'It's a picture of the current record holders.' The picture, a little fuzzy because it was thirty years old and taken with a lower quality camera than one gets today, showed a giant Yorkshire pudding so large it didn't fit into the frame. Standing before it was the bakers, all wearing their Uncle Bert's uniform and smiling proudly.

The queue moved forward, and the picture was forgotten in favour of getting to the venue.

The marquee was warmer today than it had been previously, the heat coming from the people now filling the large tent as they perused the stalls and spent their money on all manner of fine wares.

Rex lifted his nose into the air and drew in as much air as he could hold. It was filled with the scent of fine cheeses, pastry treats, meats being cooked, and all manner of conflicting odours, all of which carried the promise of a full belly if he could just get within biting range.

Looking about made Albert wonder if Alan had gotten better or worse in the night. He talked about the world record attempt and this year's Yorkshire Pudding Competition as if it were his magnum opus and it seemed cruelly ironic that he wasn't here to see how successful he had made it. Nor was Brian, of course, the person who had been usurped as the organiser by Alan. There had been a lot of bad blood between the pair, but Alan hadn't been around to shove Brian in the mixer and it certainly wasn't Brian who attacked Alan in the alleyway because that person was at least a foot taller.

Albert paused for a moment as yet again, he caught a glimpse of the truth hidden behind the mystery. There had to be something to the pair's intense dislike and what had befallen the event in the last day.

He was still pondering their rivalry when he made his way through the marquee to arrive at the tee section. To his right was mostly taken up by the world record attempt, to his left still the competition itself which was attracting a lot of interest. Dead ahead was the stage, which now had displays erected like scenery and at the front, holding the microphone was a man in a suit. He had the bearing and demeanour of a stand-up comedian and might well have been for all Albert knew. The man was in his thirties and what some might describe as a jolly fat man. He certainly had the smile for the first part and was cracking Yorkshire pudding related jokes that made his ample belly jiggle each time he laughed.

Albert listened to him for a moment but had no time for silly jokes. He turned his attention back to the competition hall. The competition was under way despite the early hour. There were ten tables with ten ovens set up in two rows of five. They were all on a raised plinth roughly a foot off the floor of the marquee which, together with a rope barrier around the outside, gave the competitors some separation from the crowds passing around them. The visitors could all watch the various teams prepare and bake their puddings which had to be made from scratch. There were to be ten heats, each with a winner advancing to a final where the panel of judges, including Ethan Bentley, would select a grand winner to receive the coveted award.

Coveted: there was a good word. Albert thought the word in his head without considering why but then realised how well it fit. Was ten thousand pounds and the chance to make a lot more enough to kill for? It was discussed last night with the police, but they all knew it was. Each of them was a seasoned law enforcement officer and had seen more terrible crimes committed for worse reasons than a life changing amount of income.

Who would replace Alan on the judging panel? There was another question. He wandered forward into the competition hall, allowing himself to be amazed at the different things the bakers were doing. Yes, they were all going after the grand prize, but there were other categories to win as well as Alan argued yesterday. On the first table, the contestants, a husband and wife from the way they were bickering Albert judged, were crafting a swan from Yorkshire puddings. It was surprising how they could get the proportions so accurate using a floppy batter product. He moved on.

On the next table, he saw more of the sweet treats he tried yesterday, and then, to his great surprise, saw that the woman hand-piping whipped cream into her Yorkshire puddings was the lady from the very café by the station he'd eaten in.

Behind him, at the previous table, the bickering turned to an argument.

'I thought you said the swan was done,' snapped the woman.

'It is, love,' replied the man, not looking up.

His dismissive tone just made the woman more angry. 'Then why does it only have one wing? Did the other fly away?' she demanded.

The man stopped what he was doing, angrily putting his spatula down to glare at her. 'What are you talking about, you daft old cow?'

Albert wasn't sure whether it was the direct insult or the result of pressure from the competition, but the woman picked up the swan with a torrent of expletives and started tearing Yorkshire puddings from it to use as projectiles.

As a sudden sinking feeling arrived in the pit of his stomach, Albert's head and eyes snapped downward to look at Rex.

The dog, happily chewing the last piece of the swan's wing, swallowed, licked his lips, and gave his human a wag of his tail. 'Whatever these things are, I like them.'

Albert quickly glanced around to see if anyone was looking and tugged the dog away on a very short lead just as the competition adjudicators were stepping in o save the man from his wife.

Circling away from them, he found Gary waiting for him at the entrance to the competition wing of the marquee.

'Dad?' prompted Gary, wondering what his father was up to this time. 'The world record bakers are this way.'

Albert had been wandering around the competition hall for more than a minute, ideas running around his head. Given the time, the competitors he could see now were most likely the first heat of the day. They had still drawn a small crowd of onlookers, but that wasn't what Albert was looking at. His eyes were drawn to one team, the one who yesterday he heard getting vocal about how they were going to win.

He tried to remember their names. However, before he could dredge them from his memory, Gary said, 'I don't believe it,' in a tone that made Albert question what it was his son could not believe. He couldn't stop his curiosity getting the better of him, and as his head turned to see where Gary was looking, he had to admit that he too, couldn't believe it.

Talking to the jolly comedian, taking a short break from his monologue of Yorkshire pudding jokes, was Alan Crystal.

They were making their way through the crowd of people when Alan shook the comedian's hand and started to move away.

'He looks surprisingly well,' observed Gary, echoing Albert's thoughts.

Albert raised his free hand, 'Alan Crystal,' he called loudly. His voice carried but in the press of people, Alan wasn't able to pinpoint where the shout had come from. It was enough to make him stop and look around for the source though, so when Albert called again, he was almost facing the right direction and raised his own hand to accompany the smile that spread across his face.

He looked very much the part of the ringmaster with a blazing red jacket and waistcoat above a pair of fitted black trousers. If his intention was to be easily spotted, he was wearing the right outfit for it.

'Gentlemen,' he greeted them. 'So lovely to see you again. You may be marvelling at how rested and well I look following last night's bout of unpleasantness.'

'You do look fully recovered,' Gary observed.

'It would seem I accidentally ingested something that disagreed with me,' Alan told them with a beaming smile. They gave me something to clear my system and I have to say, I haven't had a night's sleep that good in years. I awoke this morning feeling ready to take on the world, and in the mood to break a world record,' he added.

Albert admitted, 'Well, I must say I was not expecting to see you today.'

Alan started toward the world record attempt end of the marquee. 'Shall we? I am led to believe you came to the rescue last night when poor

Brian tried to put a stop to our most popular attraction. Terrible business of course,' Alan changed his expression to one of a suitably sombre nature when discussing his opponent's death. 'I cannot imagine who would want to do him any harm.'

Albert and Gary both frowned. 'You can't?' asked Albert. 'I was only here for a few hours yesterday and to me it seemed there were several people who might wish ill of him, you included.'

Alan looked horrified at the suggestion. 'We tussled verbally, I admit, but I would never stoop to hurting the man.' As the idea that he might be a suspect occurred to him, he said, 'I suppose I should be glad I have an airtight alibi: I was in hospital with plenty of witnesses when he was being murdered.'

'Yes, you were,' said Albert, wondering if perhaps that was awfully convenient. After all, the word accomplice wasn't one that had just been invented. Alan was friendly towards them, had been since Rex chased off his mugger and perhaps it was nothing but gratitude driving the event organiser to invite him in with a VIP pass. Albert had always been wary of coincidence though, and as he thought that thought, his eyes came to see the loose thread on the back of Alan's jacket sleeve. Little tendrils of black cotton flapped with the motion of air where a button ought to be. Albert watched as Alan's arm swung forward with the motion of his passage and then back again, giving him a clear shot of the line of buttons on his cuff. Where there ought to be four, there were only three.

Albert was asking the question before he even realised he'd decided to. 'What was the money for, Alan?'

Gary shot his father a look, but Albert's eyes were on the museum curator who flinched physically before composing himself and giving Albert a broad smile.

'You're talking about the contents of the briefcase, yes? Of course you are. It's the prize money for the competition,' Alan boasted proudly. 'I know it's more usual to give a cheque, but cash has such visual impact, don't you think.'

'It looked like more than ten thousand,' Albert insisted.

Alan just tilted his head and turned down his mouth in a what-can-I-tell-you pose. 'That's how much it was. How the mugger knew about it, I have no idea. I'm just glad you happened along when you did.'

Alan hadn't stopped walking, and content that he'd given an acceptable answer to Albert's question, he went back to chattering, gushing about how this was the most successful annual competition they had ever held. He was already reconsidering his decision to only hold the reins once, he revealed. Since leadership could not return to Brian, perhaps it was Alan's solemn duty to remain at the helm. His tone, when mentioning Brian became suitably sombre, yet only for a moment. Then he was back to chattering excitedly about planning next year's event and wondering how they could ever make it bigger and better than this one. 'It's a shame poor Brian is gone,' he joked at one point. 'I would be doing myself a favour to hand the reins back to him rather than trying to top this myself.'

Albert didn't think the man's death was cause for amusement, not that he was really listening to what was being said; he was thinking about the button they found last night under the eggs in the refrigerated storage container and how it was exactly the same as the ones on Alan's jacket. He felt an instant desire to broach the subject immediately, to grab Alan's arm and twist it around to reveal the missing button, but at this stage what was he going to accuse him of? He was the organiser of the event and the man behind the world record attempt. All the button proved was that Alan had been in the container with the chilled ingredients.

Quelling his need to know more, Albert quickly forced a smile onto his face when Alan glanced his way. 'The chaps have been working so hard to make up for lost time, they will all deserve a holiday once this is over.' He made the comment because they were coming into earshot of the bakers.

Their mood, which had taken a few blows in the last day, was better than it might have been, but not as chipper as when Albert stumped up to buy the replacement ingredients the previous evening.

Alan called out to them, 'Where's my team of record breakers?'

Heads that had not been looking his way turned to see who was calling, and he got a few weary waved hands.

'Are we still on track?' he asked.

The question hadn't been aimed at anyone in particular, and Albert had to wonder who might have stepped in to take over as their leader now that Beefy was out of the picture. Was Suzalls the next person to naturally gravitate to the top? She had seemed to be one of the more confident ones yesterday, speaking for the group when she had an opinion. Albert looked around for her, squinting a little when he couldn't find her.

The baker nearest Alan, who one might have expected to answer, was looking about for someone else to field the question. Over by the mixing machines — three now not four, which wouldn't be helping their efforts any — one of the chefs stopped loading ingredients and came forward.

He looked tired, and when he came close enough for Albert to read the name embroidered on his jacket, Albert knew why: he was Dave 2 and had been here since midnight.

'Good morning, Mr Crystal,' he acknowledged the organiser in a lacklustre I'll-talk-to-you-but-I-hope-you-appreciate-you-are-stopping-me-from-doing-the-one-thing-you-want-me-to-do subtext.

'How are things proceeding?' Alan repeated his question. 'Are you on track to have the pudding ingredients ready on time?' The anxiety in Alan's voice was palpable.

Dave 2 nodded. 'Just about, yes. Those who didn't work through the night, were here early this morning to lend a hand. We're really short on people.'

'Why?' asked Alan. 'I know you are missing Beefy, but surely you can cope with the loss of one member of the team.' He said it in the way that managers everywhere use on workers when they have no idea nor interest in understanding how complex a task might be. The workers were supposed to do it – just get it done and don't waste my time with excuses just because I have asked you to do the impossible.

Dave 2 snorted, a small escape of air from his nose: he'd been spoken down to like that before. 'Well, Mr Crystal, it's not just Beefy we are missing, several of the team didn't come back this morning. I think word of the second murder put them off. We could do with some extra hands, but that's not really the issue.'

Alan's tone turned impatient. 'What is then?'

'The oven,' Dave 2 replied, making air quotes around the word oven. It's lit, but it's all guess work now.'

'Guess work?' asked Alan, concern creeping into his voice and his face.

Dave 2 looked around as if checking to see who might be here to back him up and found himself very alone. 'Well, yes, Mr Crystal. Did no one explain this?'

Alan's hands clung to each other like friends about to receive bad news and looking to each other for support. 'Explain what?' he begged in a terrified voice.

Dave 2 now looked worried himself. 'There's no experience to draw on, Mr Crystal. We make Yorkshire puddings in a nice clean factory. The temperature in the factory is controlled, the temperature in the oven is controlled and inside the oven the temperature is the same all over. We are going to attempt to bake this giant Yorkshire pudding in an open pan, heated from the bottom only and with the outside temperature in single figure degrees centigrade. One stiff breeze at the wrong time and we might get no rise at all. To get a good rise, the trick is to get the oil really hot so it flash-fries the batter when it hits the pan. We cannot do that.'

'Why not,' demanded Alan, still sounding horrified. It was clear none of this had been even suggested to him before.

Dave 2's brow furrowed. 'Think about it, Mr Crystal. It's one giant open pan. We can heat it and get the oil inside hot, but we cannot pour four tons of batter into the pan in one go. It will take us ten minutes or more to get all the batter in and the moment we start adding it, the temperature of the oil will drop.'

Alan stared at the man, his mouth flapping as he tried to form his next question. 'What ... what are you telling me?' he asked quietly, biting the fingers of his left hand as he waited for the answer.

Albert eyed Alan critically. He was far too invested in the outcome of the record attempt. The colour had drained from the man's face and his legs were twitching as if they were having trouble supporting him. Was he about to faint? Albert couldn't help but question what Alan had riding on the event.

Dave looked back at Alan with an open expression. 'I'm not telling you anything, Mr Crystal. I'm just saying I don't know how this is going to go. It's not like we got to do ten practice runs beforehand.'

'Oh, my goodness,' Alan was now bent at the waist and looking for something to grab to keep himself upright. As he stumbled, the something he grabbed was Dave 2 who looked shocked to be now supporting the smartly-dressed man's weight.

Gary, equally surprised to see Alan struggling, stepped forward to help take his weight. 'Can we get a hand here?' he called aloud.

The event organiser was hyperventilating, so as another of the chefs ran over with a plastic chair, Gary folded him into it and shoved his head down to get it below his heart. Holding a hand to the back of Alan's head, Gary flared his eyes at his father and whispered, 'What the heck?'

Albert didn't know the answer to that question.

'Mr Smith?' asked a voice from behind his right shoulder.

Albert swung his head to find a woman in her thirties looking up at him. She was an attractive red head, wearing designer red-rimmed glasses and a bright red designer label raincoat. Albert guessed instantly that she was one of the plain clothes officers Chief Inspector Doyle deployed to the event.

'Hello,' he replied, stepping away from the crazy drama going on with Alan Crystal. 'You were told to find me, were you?' he asked to confirm his guess.

The woman glanced down to her hands, in which she held her police identification. Albert got a second to look at it, no more, before she slipped it back into the matching red handbag hanging over her shoulder.

'My instructions were to identify myself to you and point out my colleagues.' She turned her eyes to where, at the nearest stall, one selling freshly cooked roast beef sandwiches using a Yorkshire pudding as the bread, three men stood. 'That's constables Washington, Wilshaw, and Jones,' she pointed out, identifying each in the line.

They looked to have been carved from the same mould with their matching haircuts and matching plain clothes outfits. All three made brief eye contact and turned away again, pretending to peruse the stallholder's wares.

There were four police officers here, maybe more, Albert considered as the detectives might decide to show up anyway. Like a flash of lightning, inspiration hit. 'Can you cook?' he asked.

The female police officer's head tilted to the right in question. 'Cook?'

Ninety minutes later, they were in the food preparation area of the world record attempt.

'This is not what I expected to be doing today,' complained Police Constable Wilson Wilshaw as he cracked what he guessed to be his thousandth egg.

In contrast, his colleague, the red-headed constable, Sophie Hendrix, was rather enjoying herself. 'I dunno, Wilson, I think this is kind of fun. The other two are just wandering around outside. What if these guys break the record for the biggest Yorkshire pudding? We'll have been part of that.'

'I don't even like Yorkshire puddings,' Wilson complained.

'What?' asked Albert, not believing his ears. He'd volunteered two of the officers before they knew what was happening. Hearing Dave 2 complain that he needed more hands, and knowing the police wanted to be in the thick of the action, he didn't bother to ask their opinion first. Sophie claimed she could make a mean Victoria sponge, and volunteered Wilson because she knew he grew up in a pub making food with his dad before he joined the police. 'How can you not like Yorkshire pudding?' Albert wanted to know. 'Roast beef with Yorkshire pudding is one of the most quintessentially British dishes on the planet. When other nations think about British cuisine, they picture cups of tea, cucumber sandwiches, fish 'n' chips, and roast beef with Yorkshire pudding.'

Wilson just shrugged. 'It's bland. It doesn't taste of anything.'

Albert felt like throwing something at the young man's head.

Granted untested volunteers, Dave 2 had found them easy, yet necessary, tasks to perform. It freed up some of his known bakers who were taken outside to help with the fire and the giant pan and left the two police officers in the main marquee with Albert, Gary, and others where they could watch over what was happening. The bakers' uniform of white jacket and check trousers together with the traditional white baker's floppy hat made for the perfect disguise too. They were blending in, snooping around, and watching what was going on with perfect disguises.

After the worrying news about the fragility of the record attempt, Alan took a few moments to get the colour back into his face, but once recovered he made his excuses and went back to the competition where he was required to announce a heat winner. The heats were to be judged by him alone, with the ten heat finalists going before a panel.

Each time there were cheers from the competition floor, the bakers looked up to see another team advance to the final.

'Is that next batch ready to mix yet?' called Dave 2, popping his head back through the flap of the marquee. 'I think we might have got the pan about ready. We'll have to start pouring soon either way.'

He interrupted their conversation, but they were ready with the batter ingredients which now needed to be transferred to one of the mixers as the previous mix was taken away. It was a continuous process that had been going on for over twelve hours already. Struggling to understand why they were doing it this way, Gary asked why they couldn't just use an even bigger mixture. The answer, apparently, was that it would never mix properly, leaving pockets of dry ingredients when it was essential the batter was smooth, thin, and even.

They each carried their measured, heavy buckets of ingredients to a mixer where a pair of men, looking sweaty and fatigued, were adding flour – plain not self-raising – using yet more of the same buckets. It was another top tip: use equal quantities of milk, flour, and eggs. Albert watched for a moment as a thousand eggs went into the mixer along with buckets of milk and bucket after bucket of flour. The flour went in last, added to the wet mix to minimise how much it clouded. After yesterday's debacle, no one wanted to see flour in the air.

Thinking about the 'fun' events of yesterday afternoon, Albert looked down at Rex.

Rex was bored. Or the version of bored that a dog gets when it would much rather be doing something else. To entertain himself, Rex supposed, his human had jammed a baker's hat on his head. It wouldn't stay on, but the bakers had found it amusing so joined in, finding a piece of elastic to attach to the hat and go under his chin.

He didn't much care about the hat; it wasn't bothering him, but he wanted to explore all the magnificent smells filling the air and his human wouldn't let him. In fact, the old man still seemed sore about the incident with the curtain pole and the tree. Rex did not consider any of the things that happened earlier to be his fault per se, but his human was being far more strict than usual about what he was permitted to do.

Albert was back to cracking eggs and thinking to himself that he was getting good at it. He'd started copying Wilson, who was doing it one handed and never getting any shell in his bowl. Albert had made the mistake of cracking the eggs straight into the bucket when he started and then found it impossible to get a small piece of shell out because there were too many eggs swimming around. Now, they were all using bowls – tap the egg to crack the shell, then hold it over the bowl and push in with two fingers and a thumb. Another egg deposited the white and yolk perfectly into the bowl, causing Albert to smile: he felt like a baker today even though he hadn't baked anything.

He turned his mind back to the murder investigation and to the question of Alan Crystal having an accomplice. Like a jolt of electricity, a dastardly scenario hit him. The egg in his hand banged against the side of the bowl with three times the force required, smashing the egg, and sending its contents to the floor.

'Don't mind if I do,' said Rex, moving in with a handy tongue to remove the tasty morsel as it dripped from the table to the temporary rubber matting beneath.

'The murder victim,' he blurted, getting Gary's attention along with Sophie and Wilson's. 'Does he own a moped?'

All three serving police officers stared at him for a second before Sophie took the radio from her pocket. 'I can find out,' she offered.

Gary enquired, 'Why do you ask, Dad? Is this something to do with the mugging you interrupted yesterday?'

Albert scrunched up his face. 'I'm not sure. I feel like I have missed something. We all know that Alan Crystal is acting strange, and that he was attacked by a man with a baton, and then managed to accidentally ingest something that made him terribly sick yesterday. I am beginning to wonder if the three things are connected.' He didn't mention the man in the black leather jacket; Gary was too sceptical already.

'Connected how?' asked Wilson.

All Albert could do was shrug. 'If we knew that, we might know why Brian Pumphrey went into the mixer and couldn't get out, and we might know why Jordan Banks was stabbed.'

133

With a little steel in his voice, Gary said, 'Maybe it's time we had a chat with Mr Crystal. Perhaps he can shed some light on what is going on.'

Albert eyed his son sceptically. 'Getting interested now are you, Gary? I thought you didn't want to be involved in local affairs.' Gary was about to answer, but Albert had more to say. 'I don't think we can quiz him yet: we don't know anything.'

'Jordan Banks does not own a moped,' Sophie announced. 'I suppose that doesn't mean he couldn't get hold of one, but there isn't one registered to him.'

Albert accepted the news with a nod. 'Alan Crystal was convenient with the truth about the mugging yesterday. He was carrying a large amount of cash with him, but I'm not sure I believed his explanation that it was the prize money. The mugger went for the briefcase as if he knew what was in it. There's something else too ...' he tailed off without finishing his sentence.

Gary couldn't help himself from asking, 'What, Dad? What something else is there?'

Albert's forehead pinched with annoyance at his son's tone. 'The man in the black leather jacket. I saw him three times yesterday, starting in the alley where Alan was mugged. Three is too many, especially since two of them were in the vicinity of the museum.'

Gary drew in a breath and let it go. 'You think he could be the thief?'

'What thief?' asked PC Hendrix.

Gary looked her way. 'The museum had suffered a number of thefts. Artefacts, which ought to have no value, have been stolen along with more easily shifted items such as a computer and an office printer.'

'I don't think it has anything to do with the murders,' stated Albert. 'At least, I cannot work out how to connect the two. The thief, if we focus on that for a moment, must be someone with access to the building because there is no sign of forced entry, the curator told us. The man in the black leather jacket is something different.'

'Either way,' said Gary, wiping his hands on a cloth to clean them. 'I think it's time we spoke with Mr Crystal.'

Albert was quiet for a moment, thinking about what might be missing from the puzzle. Something was, that he knew for certain, but without a clue to steer him, he didn't know which way to look. Glancing at Sophie, he asked, 'Is one of your colleagues following him?'

The answer to his question turned out to be yes, but also no. Neither officer could currently locate the man in the bright red jacket and waistcoat. It seemed ridiculous that he could be hard to find given how utterly he stood out, but that was their report. According to the other officers here in plain clothes, Alan Crystal was nowhere to be found. He was at the competition floor one moment but gone the next. They had been searching for him for several minutes with no success.

Albert didn't like that news at all. Before he could make a decision about what to do about it, Sarah, the woman with the unkempt hair and the clipboard rushed up to the edge of the world record food prep area.

'I say,' she called, waving her arm to get attention. 'I say.'

Albert looked her way, wondering what she might want so urgently and discovering it was distinctly him that she was looking at. He pointed a thumb at his own body in question.

'Yes,' said Sarah. 'You were with Alan yesterday. Have you seen him in the last few minutes? The next round of puddings needs to be judged and he seems to have vanished.' She was doing the very British thing of playing down the utter panic she felt.

Albert shook his head. 'Sorry, no. I haven't seen him in more than an hour.' That wasn't strictly true because often when he looked up, he could see the man's bright red jacket moving somewhere in the crowd.

'Bother,' she muttered, which was a posh British substitute for many words that wouldn't make it into print. 'I shall have to ask Amber to step in.' Still muttering to herself, she bustled away looking harried and stressed.

Just then, Dave 2 popped his head back through the flap of the marquee, sending a waft of cool autumn air inside. 'Is your last batch ready?'

'Last?' echoed Gary.

Dave 2 beamed. 'Yeah! That's it. The other teams,' there were four of them all making the batter to get it ready, 'are all doing their last ones too. We have enough, so now it's time to start the pour.'

'Oh, thank heavens,' said Wilson, who probably wasn't going to want eggs for breakfast for a while.

Whether it was fatigue induced madness or stress pumping adrenalin through his veins, Dave 2 was vibrating with excitement. 'If you drop that batch off at the mixer, come outside and you can see it. This is either going to work brilliantly or be a complete disaster. The oil in the pan is smoking hot now, though it's making the fire brigade a little nervous, truth be told. You know what? I think this might just work.'

The confidence he displayed now was a hundred and eighty degrees opposite to his opinion earlier when talking to Alan. Albert sure hoped he was right. It would be something to tell the grand kids, he could put a photograph on the wall, and he got to do it with his son. Swept up in the excitement of it, he put the murder investigation and whatever the heck else was going on to one side and followed Dave 2 while Gary, Sophie, and Wilson took the ingredients to the mixer.

Rex led the way as they stepped outside into the crisp autumn air, tugging at his human's arm because outside there were people he recognised.

'Rex!' said Station Officer Hamilton gleefully.

Of course, thought Albert, Dave 2 said the fire brigade were here, so it would be the local crew from just down the road. He threw them a wave that was a mix of apology for blighting their lives so many times, and yet again thanking them for their help.

Rex was bouncing on the spot with excitement. 'Come on, human,' he barked. 'It's play time. Look they're all standing around bored.'

Albert knew what Rex wanted but held onto his lead tightly while he spoke to Dave 2. 'Is it safe enough for Rex to be off the lead out here?'

Dave 2 looked around and then down at the dog. 'He won't run under the pan, will he?'

Albert looked at the giant pan for the first time. It was enormous. In fact, it was so big that enormous didn't do it justice.

Seeing the old man gawp open-mouthed, Dave 2 grinned. 'I know what you are thinking. It's the exact same size as an Olympic swimming pool,' he revealed. 'Not as deep, obviously, the lip is only eighteen inches. If we can get the rise to anywhere near the top of the edge, I think we will all call it a victory.'

Rex nudged his human's leg, bashing against the knee to make it fold.

Albert almost toppled, but the dog achieved the effect he desired. 'You want off the lead for a while do you, Rex?' Albert reached down to get the clip where the lead connected to the collar. 'Just you stay close and stay out of trouble, you hear?'

The lead came free, and Rex darted away. He remembered the game he played with the firefighters yesterday when they threw a toy around for him. To his great joy, one of them produced a frisbee today and the chase was on.

Seeing his dog streak after the whizzing disc, Albert turned his attention back to Dave 2. 'Who's the chap in the suit?' Albert asked, nodding his head at a man with a clipboard and a camera standing halfway down the righthand side of the pan.

'That's the fellow from Guinness. He got here about half an hour ago,' said Dave 2. 'If you are going to ask me what he is doing, I'm afraid I have no idea.'

The pan, giant size that it was, had hundreds of steel feet beneath it to support its great weight and keep it a foot off the ground. Underneath it were row upon row of gas burners, all rigged in lines spaced a foot or so apart. The fifty-five-yard pan must need … Albert did some math in his head and came up with a hundred and fifty or so rows. The entire operation must have cost thousands to manufacture just for this one attempt at a pointless world record. Not that Albert would label it as pointless out loud in his present company.

All along the left side were front loading dump trucks. Each of which held a huge container filled with batter. At the far end, Albert could see bakers carrying large buckets of batter fresh from the mixer. This was the last of it and soon the pour would begin.

'How long will it take to cook?' Albert asked.

Dave 2 scratched his chin. 'A normal Yorkshire pudding will rise and set in just twenty minutes. This lot … I reckon it will be a couple of hours.'

Albert was keen to see the batter poured and watch what would happen when it hit the smoking hot oil. However, he now had a two-hour window when he wasn't needed to do anything for the world record attempt and there was a mystery to solve. For starters, if Alan Crystal was missing, the first question to be answered was whether he had chosen to leave, or was, in fact, being held by someone?

Just as he started to walk over to collect Rex from the firefighters, Albert thought of something he wanted to ask Dave 2. 'I haven't seen Suzalls today, is she not here?'

Dave 2 shook his head. 'That's why I've lost Dave 1 as well.'

Albert waited for Dave 2 to expand on his statement, but nothing was forthcoming until he prompted it. 'I'm sorry, Dave. I'm not sure what you are telling me.'

'They're husband and wife, Dave 1 and Suzalls. He was here last night but took off at silly o'clock this morning. I'm not sure what it was about but his parting comment was, "I'm going to kill her." I think maybe she was playing around on him again and he was rushing home to catch her. It wouldn't be the first time,' he told Albert like he was letting him in on a big secret. Dave 2 then puffed out his chest. 'Of course, I've always thought that a woman only cheats if her man can't cut it in the bedroom. No such problems for me, I can tell you.'

Albert paid Dave 2's bragging no mind and started walking away again. Suzalls was married to Dave 1, not Beefy. So, what had he seen yesterday? The answer was obvious really, especially if the story Dave 2 told of her cheating history was fact based and not just rumour. The discovery allowed a piece of the puzzle to slot into place and that spurred Albert on.

He needed to check on a few things, and he needed to find the police officers and see what they were doing about the missing museum curator. To Albert's mind, the longer Alan stayed missing, the more likely it was something had befallen him.

Cursing himself for not pushing Alan to reveal what trouble he was in sooner, Albert called for Rex. 'Come on, boy!'

His shout got a collective, 'Awww,' from half a dozen firefighters who were bored standing around at the public event. It was one of those things that fell into their scope of duties and sounded way more fun than they actually ever turned out to be. Today they got to watch a giant tin get turned into the world's largest Yorkshire pudding. Whoopee.

Rex spun around to see his human beckoning. 'Already? I was having so much fun.'

Seeing how disappointed the firefighters were gave Albert an idea. 'I can leave him with you for a while if you like,' he offered. 'He could do with the exercise if you want to run him around for a bit.'

The firefighters turned their collective eyes toward Station Officer Hamilton who chuckled. 'Maybe he'll stay out of trouble if he's with us.'

It was a sly dig at how many times they had rescued the dog in the last twenty four hours but Albert took it in the spirit it was intended and held out Rex's lead to the nearest fire fighter.

'Take good care of him, please. He shouldn't run off, but it would be wise to keep him on the lead when you stop playing just in case.'

Rex saw the lead change hands and heard what his human said. Filled with excitement, he darted over to the old man's legs, almost jumped up at him, but stopped himself in the certain knowledge he would just knock him over if he did, and then hared back the way he came just in time for the firefighter holding the frisbee to send it on a fresh break for freedom.

Rex ran and ran, tracking it with his eyes because this wasn't a job for his nose, and watched it land on the grass. When he turned around to run back, his human was gone from sight, but Rex was with humans he knew and felt safe enough to remain with them until his human returned.

Frisbees were great because there was more than one game involved each time it was thrown. He got to chase it and bring it back, sometimes he even got to catch it by leaping into the air depending on how it was thrown. Then, he could run around the humans and have them try to catch him - he couldn't do that with his human - and when they caught him, he got to play tug with it, pitching his jaw strength against their grip.

He did that this time, feeling proud that three of the firefighters had to club together to tear it from his mouth. Then he got to chase it again.

There was a cry of dismay from behind him as the frisbee sailed over the hot pudding pan. The bakers were doing something with it that was getting them excited and Rex could smell something cooking in it now. The frisbee, which the humans seemed to think was going to land in the batter mix, sailed on over it to land on the far side. He was well away from the part of the marquee where the bakers were working, and closer to the stage in the middle of the tee now.

Rex leapt into the air and landed with his front paws pinning the evil object to the ground. However, his triumphant bark of, 'I've got you,' died in his throat when his nose picked up a scent.

It was the scent from yesterday, the truly evil one the cat's human had all over him after Rex knocked him down. Rex hadn't forgotten about the cat, but he hadn't seen it or smelled it since yesterday so maybe it was gone. The nasty chemical medicine smell was back though. Faint, but undeniable. It made him shudder once more at the memory of being given it himself.

Yesterday, he'd tried to tell his human about the medicine scent and what he thought it meant when the human in the suit got ill. He hadn't been able to make the old man understand though and that bothered him because he thought it was important. He couldn't work out what was going on, but there were two dead humans and he knew that was bad. Maybe this was something to do with it and maybe it wasn't. Either way, he let the frisbee drop from his mouth and sniffed the air.

The firefighters, who were having a great time playing with the dog, not least because it allowed them to move around and warm up a bit, were now watching the dog wander off. The frisbee had been getting thrown farther and farther each time so now the dog was almost a hundred yards away and his decision to not come back created a problem: no one wanted to tell the old man they had lost his dog.

It's a Fix, I Tell Thee!

Albert was inside the marquee where he was starting to look for any of the police officers. He couldn't even see his son. He picked his phone from his pocket, but holding it in his hand, he decided to climb onto the platform by the mixers to get a look over the crowd. The two sweaty men were no longer there, their buckets abandoned as they went to join everyone else for the pour and the anxious time that followed.

There was something going on at the big stage at the top of the tee. A crowd had gathered around the stage and more people were drifting in that direction as Albert watched. On the stage, the rotund comedian was spitting jokes and making people laugh but giving the impression he was warming them up for something or someone to follow.

Pausing briefly before phoning Gary, Albert listened to the voice booming out of the speakers dotted around the marquee. '... and then he said, it'll cost you twice that for a ferret!' the crowd burst into spontaneous laughter. Having missed most of the joke, Albert had no idea why the price of a ferret might be funny, but the comedian was done. Wafting an arm around behind him in the traditional manner of welcoming someone onto the stage, he said, 'Ladies and gentlemen, thank you for indulging my silliness. I won't keep you any longer. Here is today's biggest contributor and the man who so generously paid my cheque,' more laughter, 'only joking. I give you the man who put up today's generous prize money and the chance to have a line of goods in his stores nationwide, Ethan Bentley.'

Polite, rather than riotous applause rippled around the crowd as a handsome man in his early fifties stepped forward and into the limelight. Ethan Bentley, so far as Albert knew, was a self-made man. The story was that he and his elder brother had come up with the idea for the luxury brand supermarket chain but that his brother then died tragically only days after the foundations for the first store were cut. Ethan made his brother's baby son the replacement partner in the firm and the child was a millionaire before he started school. That was thirty years ago. Now he was a household name and appeared on his *Brilliant Business Ideas* television show every week.

Everything about him was a public relations dream come true and the current offer to give a small firm or a keen chef cooking at home the opportunity to have their wares in his stores was just another example of his keen marketing mind at work. The story would make the papers, in fact, Albert could see microphones and cameras at work at the front of the stage now – the press getting the shots and soundbites they needed.

The chatter died down as Ethan came to the front of the stage. 'Thank you, ladies and gentlemen. There's no need for me to say much, other than to wish the entrants the best of luck. I look forward to sampling some of the offerings ...'

'It's a fix!' a voice rang out from the crowd. Heads snapped around, everyone looking to see who might have spoken. The guilty person wasn't trying to hide and was now making his way through the press of people, who were parting to let him pass. 'It's a fix I tell thee!' he insisted loudly.

On the stage Ethan Bentley waited patiently for the heckler to get closer. A few feet above the heads of the crowd where he stood on the mixer loading platform, Albert got to see who it was when the crowd opened slightly to show the man. It was one of the competitors: Mr Ross of Ross Bakery, a man Albert had seen complaining to Alan Crystal the previous afternoon.

Now close enough that Ethan could look him in the eye, he said, 'I can assure you, sir, there is nothing fixed in this competition. Only the finest goods go into my stores and I shall have final say on the winning entry.'

146

Mr Ross, wearing the livery of his firm, stopped right in front of the stage. 'You'll not get to taste the best entries, Mr Bentley, because it's a fix. The winners of the so-called heats have been decided in advance somehow. You should see the abysmal monstrosity that beat my own tray of towering, crisp Yorkshire puddings in heat two. There needs to be an adjudication, I tell thee.' Mr Ross was red in the face, angry and feeling cheated, but also embarrassed by all the attention now focussed on him.

Albert remembered him distinctly, he was the owner of Ross Bakeries, the one who had been proudly showing off his puddings, yesterday. They had been towering, crisp and impressive. Had his entry today not risen as expected?

On the stage, Ethan called for calm, shushing the growing susurration of his audience. 'I believe, sir, that you should accept defeat graciously and move on. There will be many disappointed entrants today but being beaten does not mean that your version of the Yorkshire pudding is in any way diminished.'

'Beaten?' Mr Ross said as if he'd just been slapped. 'I wasn't beaten. I was cheated! It's as plain as day. Come and see for yourself, Mr Bentley. Thou's being cheated too.'

Event security were moving through the press of people, hurrying toward the troublemaker but having to do so slowly as they negotiated their way around old ladies, mothers with pushchairs, and people with dogs.

Ethan did the sensible thing and moved along. 'Thank you, ladies and gentlemen. Enjoy your day and good luck to all the competition entrants.' He turned and headed for the rear of the stage away from Mr Ross.

Security were with the vocal baker now, quietly asking him to leave but he was getting angrier by the second. 'Where's that Alan Crystal? That's who I want to speak with. Where is he? This whole thing is a fix and I paid good money to enter this competition.'

It was going to get physical if he didn't calm down soon, but Albert echoed Mr Ross's question. 'Where is Alan Crystal?' The crowd moved again, revealing Gary's location. He was talking with Sophie the redhead and one of her other colleagues here in plain clothes. It was time to join them and see what they might have discovered, but as he started down the steps from the mixer platform, he spotted someone he hadn't seen for hours.

Rosie was sitting on a plastic chair in the now abandoned world record attempt preparation area. She was all alone, apart from baby Teddy sitting on her knee, and there were tears streaming down her face.

Tears

Unable to ignore her, Albert rushed to her side. 'Whatever is the matter, Rosie? Are you hurt, did something terrible happen?'

Rosie glanced up at him, a sad, apologetic smile on her face, then looked back down again, focussing on Teddy gurgling happily on her lap. 'It's nothing really, Albert. I'm just feeling sorry for myself.'

Albert looked around until he spotted a chair, fetched it, and set it down next to her. He pulled a face at the baby. It was supposed to be a funny face that would make Teddy smile or maybe giggle, but he burst into tears to match his mother, a long wail accompanying his change in state. Albert wrote off any further thoughts about amusing the baby to focus on Rosie.

'It's clearly something,' he insisted. 'Perhaps it's something I can help with?' He did something his grandfather had taught him to do when faced with a tearful woman and produced a clean handkerchief from his pocket. Attitudes had changed a lot in the last couple of decades; women were strong and should be viewed as such. He wasn't going to argue, but a crying woman was still a crying woman in his book.

Rosie took the offered tissue, using it to dab at her eyes with one hand while shushing Teddy gently with the other. 'It really is nothing,' she claimed for a second time. 'I'm just being ridiculous.' Seeing she needed to say a little more, she explained, 'I need a job. Something steady, and I thought maybe this would turn out to be a lead into something I could do full time, or maybe even part time. It's the curse of being a single mum: I need to have Teddy so I can't work full time hours unless the job comes with a creche and few do. I pick up work here and there, like this thing with the world record attempt. The organisers were taking anyone with any kind of baking experience. It's done now though, so tomorrow, I have to go and try to find work again.'

'But surely the government provide you with benefits to support yourself and Teddy.' Albert thought about all the tax he'd paid over the years and the arguments he heard about people claiming they were better off on benefits because the government paid them so much.

Trying to calm her tears, Rosie let out a shuddering breath and allowed her shoulders to sag. 'They do. Of course they do. It just enough for me to feed and clothe the pair of us, but I live in a terrible area in a terrible flat with terrible neighbours and Teddy will have to grow up in that environment unless I can find a way to escape it. I need a decent job that I can build on. Truthfully, I took this job because I wanted to enter the competition.'

'Why didn't you?' Albert asked her.

She sniffed and dabbed her eyes again. 'I couldn't afford the entry fee,' she admitted sadly. 'My granny's Yorkshire pudding recipe would have knocked their socks off.'

Albert wanted to look for Gary and catch up on how they were getting on locating Alan Crystal. There were a dozen or more other things he could be doing that would be more productive than comforting Rosie, but her need at this very moment was greater than anything else. She looked miserable and lost, and had done since he met her yesterday, bowled over and injured during the aborted mugging.

However, her boast gave him an idea. 'You know, Rosie, I only came to York to learn how to make a decent Yorkshire pudding. Is your granny's recipe a secret? Or will you show me how to make it?'

Rosie, whose eyes had been focussed solely on the child in her lap, swung up to meet Albert's. 'You really want to see it?'

Albert nodded, getting back to his feet, and holding his arms out so she could pass him Teddy. 'I really do. It would be a terrible shame if I were to leave here without the ability to make a Yorkshire pudding for myself.'

'Well then,' said Rosie, forcing herself to brighten. 'I think I had better look for some ingredients.'

With the scent in his nose, Rex set off, his paws moving at a fast lope. Unencumbered by a human to hold him back, he found a way into the marquee but there his nose became assailed by myriad other conflicting smells.

He could hear the firefighters calling his name. They were chasing him but would want to clip him back to his lead and take him outside. He wasn't going to allow that. To his right was the competition, the bakers there feverishly whipping up the next batch of Yorkshire puddings as they entered each of the different competition options. The smells coming from it were mouth watering and very distracting. Worse yet were the stalls selling hot food, of which there were plenty. The smell of bacon and sausages had always been hard to resist, so Rex promised himself he would investigate the area around the stalls for dropped treats the moment he found the thing he was trying to track.

He moved deeper inside the marquee and out of sight of the firefighters who would burst through the door behind him at any moment. Once he deemed himself to be far enough away, he closed his eyes to focus only on his nose and drew in a large sample of air. Now he had to sift and discard all the scents he could easily identify as he looked for the one he needed to find.

There it was! An unpleasant chemical tang that had been artificially flavoured. He didn't know the name for it, and though the scent alone made his stomach queasy, he was locked on now, and would find it in minutes.

His eyes opened again, and his paws leapt into action. But no sooner had he started to home in on the source of the smell, than he caught a trace of another smell – the cat.

The cat was still here somewhere. Its human was dead, but cats didn't care too much about such things in Rex's experience. They would happily move to the next human in line. Rex bared his teeth automatically upon thinking about his local nemesis but bit his rising ire down to focus on the thing he needed to find.

Getting closer to the revolting medicinal smell brought him to the back of the stage. There were lots of people around, any of whom might decide he ought not to be there, so Rex went under the tables, keeping his belly low to avoid detection. He crept along like that, sneaking between people until he found his target. It was inside a trash receptacle.

Now that he was on top of it, the smell made him want to gag. Not because it was that revolting, it had kind of a sweet note behind the medicinal, chemical tang, but the memory of ingesting it turned his stomach each time he inhaled.

Steeling himself to do what needed to be done, Rex flipped the waste bin over with his front paw. It made a dull metallic sound as the side of the bin hit the rubber matting, and the contents spilled out over the floor. A half-eaten burger rolled out too. Rex inhaled it swiftly, certain that it had been left there just for him to find. Then, he had to use his nose to root through the debris until he could see the broken plastic bottle. The lid was still on it, but the contents were gone where it had cracked down one side.

It stank now that it was right under his nose so, holding his breath, Rex picked it gingerly up and carried it between his teeth.

Rosie turned out to be an excellent tutor. For Albert, it defied logic that she struggled to find work when she was not only capable, willing, and intelligent, but qualified also. She attended catering college and at eighteen had a worthwhile career ahead of her. Falling accidentally pregnant before she could start her first job had not been part of the plan, she sighed.

Albert wanted to condemn her foolishness, he would have been quite verbal were she one of his own children, but she was not. She never mentioned the child's father, leaving Albert to guess that she either didn't know who that was, or he was out of the picture.

Still holding Teddy, who appeared content to watch and listen to his mother, Albert focussed on her top tips. 'If you want to avoid a soggy pudding or a pudding that fails to rise there are a few basics things to remember. Firstly, use equal quantities of milk and flour to eggs – you can do this by cracking eggs into a measuring jug. Essentially this works out at around two spoons of flour and two spoons of milk per egg. Always ensure that the batter mixture is smooth and there are no lumps.' She was holding her injured right hand awkwardly but had two fingers and a thumb on the whisk and made short work of demonstrating how little effort was required to get the batter smooth.

'I should use plain flour, right?' he tried to confirm one of the things he'd heard in the last day.

'That's right,' she nodded, putting the jug down. 'The rise comes from the eggs but to get a really good rise, we want to add beer.'

'Beer?' Albert's eyebrows flew away toward the top of his skull as he echoed the word.

'Uh-huh. Beer. There's a stall selling it just over there. Do you fancy a glass? I could do with one.' She was reaching for her handbag when he stopped her.

'I shall get the drinks, my dear. We'll call it payment for the lesson if you like.'

'Are you sure?' she tried to argue. It was silly really after crying about having no money and living in a hovel but also human nature to reject charity.

Albert smiled at her. 'It would be my pleasure. Does it matter what beer?'

'Not really,' she shrugged. 'Something hoppy might be best.'

The stall serving pints in plastic glasses was busy, forcing Albert to wait his turn. It took a couple of minutes, which he spent looking around the marquee for his son. He could have used his phone but wanted to dedicate some more time to Rosie before he did. There were serving police here so if the killer were here also, they were the ones who would tackle him – if they could work out who it was first, of course. They would be looking for Alan Crystal and making appropriate enquiries he felt sure.

Served his two drinks, he turned to head back to Rosie, but his path was blocked by a man with an angry face.

'Where did Crystal go?' the man demanded, a rough-looking man enquired. His hair had been cropped-short so it was little more than bristles and he had tattoos on his hands. To match the rough look, his nose had clearly been broken at some point in the past and was rather squashed now.

Albert offered him a pleasant smile. 'Mr Crystal is the organiser, sir. He doesn't tell me where he might be going.' Albert had seen the man yesterday when he came through the tent with Alan the very first time and he got accosted by some of the contestants. He hadn't spoken to Alan directly at the time but must have seen him with Albert and now thought he could provide the event organiser's whereabouts.

'If he comes this way, you tell him to come and see me, got it?' The request was delivered with an air of menace, suggesting that failing to comply would not go well for Albert.

Albert kept his face straight and played his part. 'What should I say your name is?' he enquired politely.

This time the man jutted his head forward until it was close enough for Albert to smell his breath. 'You tell Crystal that Nelson wants to speak with him, right now. That Amber Riley woman just awarded the heat prize to someone else. Crystal was supposed to give it to me. You tell him I want my money back and he'd better pray he has it to hand.

'He'll know what that is about, will he?' asked Albert amiably, ignoring the blatant aggression.

Nelson straightened up, withdrawing from Albert's personal space, but he poked a finger in his direction. 'You just make sure you tell him.'

Nelson spun around and made his way back through the crowd leaving Albert to ponder what this latest episode might be about. He didn't wonder too hard though because things were starting to make sense.

His route back to Rosie no longer blocked, Albert carried the drinks back to her location at the world record end of the marquee. It wasn't attracting many people now that the bakers were no longer there. The people who were interested, were going outside to see the world's largest

Yorkshire pudding rise, or possibly fail to rise which left he and Rosie largely alone.

Teddy was sitting on the floor playing with a stuffed toy when Albert got back to Rosie. The bear's ear was getting a jolly good chewing and already looked soaked.

'Oh, super,' said Rosie, taking the amber coloured ale. 'This will work perfectly.' Lining up the plastic cup with the already mixed batter in the bowl, she added a small amount of beer, no more than a couple of tablespoons, Albert estimated. It got another whisking and then she put it to one side.

'It has to stand for an hour at the very least, that is an absolute must. And you must put the oven to its hottest temperature and put the tin in there for ten minutes with oil in. When you check, there should be smoke coming off the oil. If there isn't, put the tin back in. Now,' she said, putting the batter mix to one side. 'we've hit a minor snag.'

Albert looked at her face. 'A snag?'

'We don't have a tin,' she explained.

Albert looked around. 'Good point.' The record attempt had plenty of ingredients left over, enough to make several batches of Yorkshire puddings at least, but no muffin tin to make them in. 'There are stalls here selling cookware, I'm sure I can buy one for a few pounds,' he guessed.

Rosie had a different idea. 'We might be able to borrow one from someone. There are so many bakers here.'

Albert wasn't sure about that. 'I don't know. They seem to be a highly strung bunch. I think I'll just buy one instead.'

'No rush. We need to let the batter stand anyway. They've paid me to be here all day, so I can't go anywhere even though there's nothing left for me to do.'

It was then, just as Albert was thinking about how much cash he had in his wallet and what a twelve-hole muffin tin might cost, that Rex appeared.

Albert frowned. 'Hey, dog. I thought you were playing with the firefighters.'

Rex padded across to the humans and spat the offensive bottle at his human's feet. Then he backed up a foot and took a grateful breath. 'This is what the human smelled of yesterday when he was vomiting. The other human, the one with the cat, had it on him and he spilled some of it. Before he died that is,' Rex added for clarity.

'Is he talking to you?' asked Rosie, her forehead pinched in a deep frown after watching the dog look down at the bottle and back up at his human while making chuffing/barking noises the whole time.

Albert didn't know how to answer that question. He was certain Rex was trying to impart a message of some kind each time he did this thing, but he was beaten on how to work out what the message might be. To respond, he said, 'I think so. I just wish I knew what he was saying.' Licking his lips, he looked down at the plastic thing on the floor by his feet and recognised that he'd seen it before. 'You want me to look at this?' he asked Rex.

'No, dopey human. I brought it over here just to amuse myself,' Rex barked his frustration. 'Look there's writing on it. I can't read it, but you must be able to.'

'What did he say that time?' Rosie asked.

'Nothing good, I don't think,' Albert frowned. 'Honestly though, he could have been telling me he met a ballet dancer and together they won first prize in a sack race.' He had to bend right over to get down to the broken bottle on the ground, taking a pen from his pocket to scoop it rather than use his finger since it was still dripping with Rex drool. 'This belonged to Brian Pumphrey, didn't it?' Albert asked of his dog. This time he got a tail wag of approval.

Albert held the bottle at arm's length with his right arm and patted down his jacket pockets with his left.

Rosie recognised what he was doing: looking for a pair of reading glasses and moved in so she could read the label for him. The small writing was hard to read and Albert's arm was wavering about until she grabbed it to hold it still.

'The name on the bottle isn't Pumphrey she advised Albert as she read. 'It's Fluffikins.'

Albert told her, 'That's Brian's cat.'

'Okay. Well, it was prescribed by Orson's Veterinary Surgery two days ago and is something called Syrup of Ipecac. Any idea what that is?'

Albert shook his head. 'None at all.'

Rex barked. 'It's to make you sick when you've eaten something you ought not to.'

Rosie glanced at Rex, letting go of Albert's arm and shuffling Teddy from one hand to the other so she could get her phone out. The task of operating her phone still proved too difficult because her other hand was injured.

'Here,' offered Albert, holding out his hands to take the baby. Teddy stared up at his face with a blank, unreadable expression. From his look of concentration, he could have been attempting to decipher the purpose of the cosmos or, more likely in Albert's opinion, filling his nappy.

With both hands free, Rosie found Syrup of Ipecac in about two seconds. 'It's an emetic,' she read from the screen of her phone. Her expression showed that she didn't know what an emetic was, which Albert thought was about right because he had no idea either. 'It says here an emetic is used to induce vomiting and that its use is limited to animals. It was found to cause long term stomach irritation in humans and ceased to be administered as a drug for human consumption in the sixties.'

Albert felt a smile tug at the corners of his mouth as another piece of the puzzle slotted into place. Now he had about as many pieces of the puzzle – sticking with that analogy – in place as he still had to locate. In his experience, once he got the first few things worked out, the rest quickly became obvious.

A flurry of movement brought Albert's eyes up to see several firefighters converging on him. They saw Rex in the next second and all showed relief.

'He got away from us,' said one.

'He was chasing the frisbee and just kept on running,' claimed another.

They all looked embarrassed and guilty at letting the old man's dog escape them, but Albert waved them into silence. 'This morning you had to rescue him from a tree for me. I know what a pickle he can be. Does someone have his lead?'

Yet another firefighter stepped forward with Rex's lead. Albert handed Teddy back to his mother, who took one sniff of him and declared him ripe. Albert was glad he didn't have to deal with it - it was bad enough picking up after Rex. With his hands free again, he took the offered lead and clipped it to his dog's collar. He gave the clever German Shepherd an ear scratch and a pat on his meaty shoulders. 'Rex, I think you found a very useful clue.'

Rex tilted his head to one side as he listened and repeated something he'd said earlier. 'This is what the human regurgitated everywhere yesterday. I think the cat's human gave it to him.'

'There he goes again,' said Rosie. 'It's so strange how he does that and never breaks eye contact until after he's finished *speaking*. What do you think he said that time?'

Albert shrugged. 'Probably saying that he knows who did what to whom and I would too if I would just use my nose.'

Rex almost fell over in shock. However, as he thought about hamming it up and mockingly falling down to play dead from a heart attack, his nose caught another familiar smell. It made his head whip around to the side and he jumped up to an alert stance facing down the length of the marquee.

Sniffer Dog

Seeing Rex sniff the air, Albert slapped his hand to his forehead – why hadn't he thought of it before? The cops are off looking for Alan Crystal but standing not two feet away was a trained police dog capable of following a scent on command. All he needed was a piece of clothing the missing man had worn recently. Albert was ready to bet money Rex would find him.

It was time to stop dilly-dallying and get to it. 'Rosie,' he addressed her as he swung his body around to face her, 'I need to attend to some matters. I'll be back in a short while with a muffin pan to use. Is that okay?'

She had Teddy under one arm and her changing bag of accessories and spare nappies over her shoulder. She was leaving to find somewhere away from the food preparation areas to deal with his stinkiness. 'Of course. I'll be around for hours yet and it's best to let the batter sit.'

'Good. I think it's high time Rex and I found Alan Crystal and got the truth from him.' He didn't add how uncertain he felt that Alan was still alive.

Setting off with Rex, Albert thanked the firefighters and left them to return to their duties. He was heading for the museum, where he believed he would find what he sought.

That wasn't where Rex was heading though. He'd caught a trace of the moped scent, a smell which he associated with two failed games of chase and bite. He also pegged the human with the moped scent as the one responsible for stabbing the other human last night. The smell was elusive, there one second but gone the next which made it impossible to track. He kept pausing to concentrate but his own human wanted to get to somewhere.

'Come along, Rex. There's a good boy,' urged Albert. 'We need to find Gary and the police officers. We have questions for them. Then we need to see if Mr Crystal got changed here, which I think he did.'

Rex heard what his human said, but he was still trying to catch the smell again. 'I don't have questions for the humans,' he replied over his shoulder. 'Mostly, I have answers for them.' He couldn't find the scent, and that meant he couldn't hope to follow it. When his human tugged his lead again in a meaningful way, Rex capitulated and went with him.

Albert kept his eyes open for any sign of Gary, then remembered his phone and cursed his stupidity. Taking it from his pocket, he cursed himself again: it was dead. Yet again he forgot to charge it last night. Remembering to do so was like a black hole in his memory and he could only ever remember to do it when he was nowhere near his charger. Angrily, he stuffed the worthless, yet expensive, piece of electronic hardware back into his pocket and pressed on.

It was well after noon now, and Albert's stomach was beginning to protest its emptiness. He would get to it soon enough, perhaps on his way back through the marquee, Albert thought as he reached the far end where it entered from the museum.

There were still people arriving, doubtless timing their visit to see the conclusion of the record attempt and the competition. Albert was forced to wait with Rex until the press of people coming in died down a bit.

Back inside the museum, the constant babble of background conversation dropped sharply away, the visitors inside the building talking in the hushed tones one associates with such places. Albert made his way to the ticket office at the front where the morose, world-weary looking man was still silently handing out tickets.

Albert rapped smartly on the glass of his booth. 'Hello, I'm looking for Alan Crystal's office, can you help me?' he enquired, fixing the man with what he hoped was an engaging smile.

The man didn't even look his way, he just jerked a thumb. 'Corridor on your left, third door on the left.' Then he punched the button to produce another ticket for the next person in line and went back to contemplating suicide or whatever else might be going through his mind.

Albert found the office easily enough, but also found it to be locked. 'Of course it's locked,' he said out loud to himself. The museum was full of people, anyone with an ounce of sense would lock their office door.

'Mr Smith?' Albert turned to see Chief Inspector Doyle approaching. On his shoulder was a taller and much younger man, his driver/assistant officer no doubt. 'Is that the curator's office?' CI Doyle asked.

Albert showed his surprise. 'Yes. I believe it is. Are you aware that he is missing?'

'That's one of the reasons I am here, Mr Smith,' the chief inspector confided. 'That, and because I am curious about this key. He held a mortice key aloft. A small tag hung from it, the type one might use at a business with a lot of keys if they were hung inside an organiser alongside each other. 'It was in Brian Pumphrey's personal effects taken from his body.'

Albert stood back as the chief inspector approached the door. One glance was all it took to confirm the lock was a mortice type - fitting for a building this old.

It slid in and turned with ease, begging someone explain what Brian was doing with a key. The door swung inward to reveal the office within, and the senior police officer wasted no time hanging around outside, striding directly through the door to stop in the middle of the room.

The younger police officer indicated Albert should go first, but Albert thrust out his hand, 'Albert Smith,' he introduced himself.

'Constable Ferris,' he replied, gripping Albert's right hand firmly.

Inside the office, Albert looked around, letting his eyes take in as much as possible before moving to inspect an empty coat hanger clinging to the edge of a bookcase. Thinking aloud, he said, 'I believe Alan Crystal is in some kind of trouble.'

'Go on,' replied the chief inspector who appeared to be doing much the same as Albert in that he was looking around the room.

Albert let his eyes track downward to the carpet, where he found a piece of black cotton. He could see it when standing but knew if he got down to the floor to pick it up, he would need his reading glasses just to find it. Instead, he motioned for PC Ferris to assist.

'You've found something, sir?' Ferris enquired.

'I rather think I have,' Albert replied. Thankful that the carpet was sky blue, which made the small piece of cotton easy to spot, he had the constable collect it with a pair of tweezers. Held up to the light, they could see that it was holding the shape it had been in; looped around and around on itself. It had relaxed slightly, but Albert knew what he was looking at. He shuffled his feet around until he was facing Alan's desk. 'Is there a pair of scissors on the desk?'

Curious, Chief Inspector Doyle looked himself, finding a pair with orange handles poking from an ornate pot of pens and other stationery paraphernalia. Reaching for them he asked, 'You need to cut something?'

Albert barked a warning. 'Don't touch!' It made the chief inspector freeze. 'I believe you may find a set of fingerprints on them that ought not to be there,' Albert advised. When CI Doyle pinched his eyebrows together, clearly wanting to hear more, Albert said, 'The piece of cotton is from a button that came from the jacket Alan Crystal is wearing today. There is more than one crime taking place simultaneously and Mr Crystal is at the centre of them all. You may wish to bag both the cotton and the scissors as evidence.'

'You are being cryptic, Mr Smith. Explain yourself, please,' the chief inspector didn't like being in the dark, and certainly hadn't liked being caught in a schoolboy error in front of his constable when he almost touched the scissors.

Albert exhaled through his nose, thinking to himself. 'Food or drink,' he muttered.

Chief Inspector Doyle frowned again. 'Excuse me?'

Albert crossed the room to look in the bin but then stopped himself and looked to Rex. 'Rex, is there anything in this room that smells of Syrup of Ipecac?'

Now CI Doyle's tone turned incredulous. 'You're asking the dog questions?'

When Albert acquired Rex as a pretend assistance dog, he had no idea what skills he came with, or if he was getting a good dog, or a duff one. All he really knew was that Rex would be well trained and obedient, which he was. Increasingly though, Albert was coming to suspect that Rex was something else, something … special.

Rex did not require a fresh sample of air to know the horrible medicine wasn't here. How to convey that message though?

Albert tried something. 'Bark if there is, Rex.'

Rex stayed silent.

'Well that's scientific proof right there,' CI Doyle remarked sarcastically.

Albert ignored him. 'Rex, if you think Alan Crystal was poisoned with Syrup of Ipecac bark once.'

The loud bark in the small office made all three men jump.

'You've finally got it!' Rex exclaimed. 'He stank of it, and it was all over the cat's human.'

The chief inspector was eyeing Albert dubiously. 'Come now, Mr Smith. I have no time nor patience for parlour tricks. We are investigating a double murder. This is no place for silliness and games.' Shifting his attention to his constable, he said, 'Ferris get crime scenes in here. I want this placed pulled apart. If there is something here, I want it found.'

Albert expected as much from the chief inspector. To anyone else … anyone who wasn't Albert Smith, Rex's behaviour would just seem like a dog doing tricks. Albert knew otherwise but he wasn't going to waste time trying to make people believe him. The chief inspector was starting to move toward the door when Albert got his attention with a single bold statement.

'I think I know what happened to Brian Pumphrey.'

Aligning the Clues

When he made the statement, Albert wasn't looking at the police officers. Ferris was dutifully following his boss to the door, but both men stopped before they left the office. Albert's attention was on the jotter pad on Alan's desk where a series of numbers and words had caught his eye.

The note made no sense that Albert could see, but he also doubted it was random. All written in the same shade of pen and in cascading lines as if written in one go, Albert believed it meant something. Had it been jotted notes, added sporadically as Alan found need to, they would be less neat.

The fifth line down held his gaze – *combi 100*. It had been underlined twice. Above it was *record 2* and above that *winner 6*.

There were more lines, some of which were just numbers.

'Mr Smith!' The chief inspector's voice cut through Albert's concentration, making him realise the senior police officer had been calling his name and getting ignored for better than thirty seconds.

Albert looked across the room. 'I'm sorry, what were you saying?'

A flash of annoyance crossed Chief Inspector Doyle's face though he remained polite and even tempered when he replied, 'You made a bold statement, sir. If you know what happened to Brian Pumphrey, you are obliged to share it with me.'

Albert nodded his understanding and scratched his chin. 'Have your officers located Alan Crystal yet?'

'That is not an answer to my question, Mr Smith,' snapped the chief inspector, losing his cool.

Knowing that he was pushing his luck, Albert said, 'All in good time, Chief Inspector. I think we should dedicate our efforts to finding the missing person.' Albert heard Doyle's snort of irritation and impatience, but using a handkerchief, he opened drawers on the desk until he got to the big one at the bottom where he found Alan's folded clothes.

To change into the red jacket and waistcoat waiting for him on the hanger, he would have needed to take off what he was wearing previously. Now Albert had the means to track the missing person. Finding him relied upon him being close enough for Rex to pick up his scent and follow it, but as he held a neatly folded shirt under Rex's nose, he suspected Alan hadn't gone far at all.

Rex sniffed deeply. This was another game the police handlers had taught him at the training academy. It wasn't his favourite game, largely because he didn't get to chase or bite anyone, but tracking was still fun, and he always got a reward when he found the target. Back then, it was usually a sock or something similar he was expected to find. However, his human wanted him to find the owner of the shirt today.

'Go on, boy,' Albert encouraged. 'Sniff him out.'

Rex started for the door, intending to go right between the two humans blocking it. However, his human held him back.

'I'm waiting, Mr Smith.' The chief inspector thought of himself as a patient man, but the shenanigans with the dog, and then the claim that he knew … what? Who killed Brian Pumphrey? The old man said he knew what happened, which was not the same thing. Regardless, whatever he knew, he needed to share.

Albert only held Rex back for a heartbeat, then urged him on again, letting the dog muscle his way past the police officers' legs as he said, 'It will all make a lot more sense once we find Alan Crystal.' With Rex tugging him along the corridor and back toward the marquee, Albert had to walk sideways to say, 'I believe you will leave here with a killer in custody, Chief Inspector. Have no fear.'

Then he and Rex were gone from sight and the chief inspector had to hurry after him.

Almost the instant he re-entered the marquee, Albert bumped into Gary.

'God, Dad, where have you been? I've been calling and calling.'

Albert was glad to see his son, and sorry he'd missed his calls. 'My battery is dead,' he showed him the phone with its lifeless screen. 'Sorry, kiddo. Any luck finding Alan?'

Gary shook his head. 'None at all. The team have split up, but also called in help. I'm expecting their chief inspector to turn up any moment.

CI Doyle chose that moment to arrive with his constable on his shoulder as usual. They were hurrying because they'd lost sight of the old man and his dog and got caught behind a family pushing their grandparents along in wheelchairs.

'Ah, here they are now,' said Gary. 'I think they were sending someone to his house as well.'

Albert rubbed the tip of his nose. 'I think Alan is here. Mr Crystal is heavily invested in today's outcome.'

Gary wanted to know what his father meant by that, but Rex was tugging at his lead and Albert was on the move again.

Rex chose to guess where he might pick up the target's scent. It lingered everywhere in the museum, which wasn't helpful, but it was also faint and fading – Rex could tell the difference between a residual scent and the source. In the marquee, he sampled the air, reaching out with his strongest sense to filter out all the background smells and found a trace of the moped scent again. Annoyed, he pushed it to one side to focus on his job. If the target was here, Rex would find where he had been and from there, in theory, be able to track him. His human had stopped to talk to his son, which gave Rex a chance to close his eyes and examine the air.

When he found what he wanted, his eyes snapped open and his legs started moving: it was go time.

Albert felt the lead go taut just a half second before his arm was yanked forward. If he didn't go with it, he was going to stumble and fall. Rex was doing what he'd been asked to – he was tracking Alan Crystal.

Moving through the crowd inside the marquee, the dog was on a mission, weaving through legs and around people with a determination that made Albert bump off half the people he needed to pass. After apologising to a dozen people and almost falling over a pushchair, Albert had to dig his feet in and haul Rex back to slow him down. 'I can't go that fast, Rex.'

Rex didn't want to slow down; he was excited by the game and looking forward to his reward. However, appreciating that his human was no longer a pup, he slowed his pace, using the extra time to check around for more of the moped smell. What he got instead was blood. Just like last night, the metallic tang of blood hung heavy on the air. It wasn't close by, but it was there, it was fresh, and it was human. It also hadn't been there a moment ago.

What Albert noticed as they made their way through the press of people in the marquee was that they weren't really moving through them at all. It was more a case of moving with them as the crowd moved of its own accord, all more or less in the same direction.

Going with the flow, Albert and Rex, together with Gary, the chief inspector and other police officers who had spotted them and tagged on, were swept through the marquee, past the stage, and out through a now open flap at the back to the grass outside where people were gathering.

Someone nudged Albert's shoulder on their way outside, squeezing through a gap too small for them to fit but making it through anyway. It was a man in his twenties he saw, one arm trailing behind to where he held the hand of a pretty young girlfriend. 'They actually did it!' he gushed to her as they passed him.

The young woman mumbled an apology as she too rushed through the narrow gap. What *they* had actually done confused Albert for a moment, until his brain caught up to inform him the two hours of baking time had elapsed, and the world's biggest Yorkshire pudding attempt was a success.

A small platform could be seen ahead of them. It wasn't there earlier – it was where the trucks with all the pudding mix had been for the pour – yet the hastily erected stage now contained several elated-looking bakers, Sarah from the event committee, and the man from Guinness. The man from Guinness was shaking hands with Dave 2 for the cameras, flashes popping to illuminate them in the mid-afternoon glow.

Rex tugged at Albert's arm, trying to pull him to the left. The blood and the target scent were both in this direction. He leaned with his low body weight as his human leaned the other way to stop him. Obediently,

Rex stopped his tugging, pausing his search so his human could do whatever it was he was doing.

Albert had wanted to get into the pictures being taken, yet it no longer seemed important in the wider scheme of what was happening. Despite that, Albert found himself staring at a poster erected to the side of the small stage.

'Dad, what's happening?' asked Gary, wondering why his father was holding Rex back.

Albert gritted his teeth. The poster was a blown-up version of a photograph in the museum, the shot of the previous world's largest Yorkshire pudding. He needed to get a closer look at it but there was no way through the crowd, and he needed to let his dog continue tracking.

He didn't bother to explain why he had stopped, choosing instead to make a mental note to check it shortly when the chance arose. With a click of his mouth, they set off again. 'Find him, Rex. Good dog,' Albert encouraged.

Needing no such motivation, Rex put his nose to the ground and let it guide his paws. The scent was getting stronger, but right then, when he knew he was closing in, the scent of the moped caught his nostrils again. His nose did a double take, filled with surprise because the two scents were intertwined. They were in the same direction!

Rex increased his pace, Albert wailing for him to slow, then giving up and passing the lead to Gary so he and the younger generations could chase on after the dog.

Rex followed his nose, constantly checking the direction by moving his nose to the left and right. Like a metal detector, the scent would fade each time he moved it away from the correct track. The target was back here somewhere, away from the marquee and in between the vans, trucks, and storage containers at the rear of the venue.

Onward through the first line of vehicles, then the second, the scents of blood, the moped and his target getting stronger with every step. Then he found them, just as he suspected, all three in the same place inside a shipping container. Rex strained at his lead, listening to the voices coming from the other side of the container's door.

Gary was flanked by officers on either side, the four younger plain-clothes officers at the front but the chief inspector and his constable keeping pace just as easily. A glance behind reassured him that his father was coming, but their chase appeared to have reached its destination. The dog was panting heavily through excitement and exertion, indicating the container but being held back by Gary. He was no dog handler, but Gary had seen the K-9 units operate many hundreds of times so knew that Rex had found his target.

Wordlessly, he indicated to the other officers for silence, and pointed to the container with a flat palm.

They all got it, the trained and disciplined officers fanning out to either side, ready to go in. None were armed, that's just not the British way, so Gary hoped whoever was inside wasn't armed either.

They could see the container's door wasn't locked, just pulled almost closed. There were voices coming from inside, and though they echoed so much in the enclosed metal box the people outside could not make out what was being said, the terrified urgency in the tone could not be missed.

Gary, knowing he was the ranking officer, held up his hand, checked he had eye contact with all the other officers as they stood poised for action, then counted down with his fingers and said, 'Go!'

Wilshaw was nearest, taking his cue and yanking the door open. It swung wide to reveal the unlit interior. It was starkly devoid of goods inside; whatever had been brought to the venue in it was now deployed elsewhere, but what it did contain was three people. As a group, the officers bundled through the door, using shock tactic and the element of surprise to minimise the risk to themselves.

Wilshaw, right at the front, was the first to speak, his words a whispered muttering. 'What in the world?'

Gary held Rex back by the entrance to the container, waiting for his father to catch up, but the police officers couldn't hold off – they were needed urgently!

Alan Crystal was chained to a loop in the roof of the container where he hung limply. His feet were on the floor, but he was sagging as if unable to support his own weight. He'd taken a severe beating, it seemed though not to his face, which was unmarked. On the floor, by his feet was a large man. He wore a black leather jacket and dark jeans over grubby running shoes. His neck was so thick it didn't really exist. He wasn't moving. At all.

Rex's growl took everyone by surprise. His hackle was standing on edge, creating a line of fur running down his spine as he threatened with words no one else could understand. 'Try escaping me this time.' The dog's focus was on the third human in the dark space, the one holding the large wooden mallet. He stank of the moped, it was in his clothes and on his body, and Rex knew it was the same human he'd chased and lost twice now.

Rex growled again. He had the moped human cornered now. He wouldn't hurt him, but if the human chose to run, he would chase, and he would most definitely bite.

Gary tugged the dog back, looking down as he wondered what could be making the dog growl like that. 'Quiet, Rex,' he tried, using a commanding voice.

Hearing the command, Rex looked up in question. 'Quiet? He's the killer, you daft human!'

The police officers were rushing forward, barking orders as they closed in on the man holding the mallet.

'Drop it!' ordered PC Wilshaw, his tone demanding compliance with an unspoken side order of 'or else' tagged on.

Albert wheezed to a stop, one hand on the side of the container to support himself while he got his breath back.

The mallet clattered noisily to the steel floor, the sound it made echoing loudly in the confined space. The man who had been holding it looked ready to faint, his face white with shock and disbelief.

'He saved me,' Alan managed to croak. Wilshaw and Hendrix were about to tackle the man with the mallet to the floor thinking him to be the attacker. Alan's gasped sentence changed that.

Albert, leaning against the doorframe to get his breath back, saw the hastily advancing officers alter their stances. Then, looking down, Albert saw the man in the black leather jacket lying on the cold steel floor and recognised him. Earlier Gary asked if Albert thought he was their thief, and Albert argued but couldn't say why. Seeing him now, it was obvious his motivation was more to do with Alan than it was the museum, and he had a reasonable idea what it was.

Hendrix dealt with the white-faced man, guiding him gently backward until he was using the wall of the container for support, then making him bend from the waist to get his head lower than his heart. 'What's your name?' she asked.

Still bent at the waist with the redhead supporting his shoulders, came his muffled reply, 'Lee Oliver.'

The name made Albert scrutinise the man more closely. It was dark inside the container, but there was enough light for Albert to see that he knew the young man; he was one of the competitors, here with his father from Oliver's Bakery – the bunch from Wetherby. Albert scratched his nose in thought.

Meanwhile Wilshaw and Washington freed Alan from his bindings. He collapsed into Wilshaw's arms, the strong, young officer having to take his entire bodyweight until Washington pitched in. Together they lowered him to a seated position on the floor next to the chief inspector and his constable, Ferris, who were checking the condition of the third man.

Ferris looked up from checking the man's pulse with a negative expression on his face. 'No pulse,' he announced quietly. With Chief Inspector Doyle giving the commands, they made to flip him onto his back to give CPR but when they attempted to move him, his head flopped at an impossible angle.

'Did I kill him?' asked Lee Oliver with Hendrix quietly. His words were full of remorse, killing the man hadn't been his intention. 'I only hit him once.'

'You're a hero,' Alan proclaimed from his position sitting on the dirty floor.

The chief inspector got back to his feet. 'I shall need statements from you both once you are recovered enough.'

Ferris was fishing around inside the dead man's jacket, looking for a wallet. Finding it in the right back pocket of his jeans, Ferris flipped it open, checked the picture on the driver's license against the figure on the floor and said, 'Warren Bradley. Anyone know the name?'

The chief inspector did. 'He's a nasty piece of work. Last I heard he was doing time for breaking arms. He used to do debt collection work, the type where he cuts off pinky toes as motivation to cough up.' He was looking directly at Alan, when he asked, 'What did he want from you, Mr Crystal?'

'He wanted me to give him the prize money,' Alan stuttered, still holding his gut. I think he's been following me, actually. I'm sure I spotted him once or twice in the last few days.' Albert made a mental note but didn't say anything. 'He grabbed me when I went to the gents,' Alan snivelled, the memory of his attack affecting his emotions. 'He put something over my mouth, chloroform maybe. All I know is I woke up in here and he kept hitting me. I thought he was going to kill me, until I saw Lee creeping through the door with the mallet in his hands.'

'How did you come to be here?' CI Doyle asked, his eyes pinning Lee Oliver to the spot.

Looking terrified, Lee gulped. 'My dad is entered in the competition. I just came outside for a cigarette. He was hitting Mr Crystal when I found them,' Lee said. 'The big man, that is. I could hear something happening inside, it sounded like a fight but when I saw what it was, I knew I had to do something to help.'

'Why didn't you call for help?' the chief inspector wanted to know.

The man was still bent over slightly and leaning against the interior wall of the container. He gave a half shrug. 'I was going to, but I knew it would give me away and I couldn't be sure anyone would hear me. I spotted the mallet on the ground outside, I guess it was used to hammer in the marquee pegs.'

Albert had his breath back and a bucket of questions so full that it was threatening to overflow. Before anyone else could speak, he pushed off from the door frame, taking Rex's lead from Gary's hand, and moved into the container. He'd been watching Rex whose eyes hadn't left Lee Oliver at any point. He knew his dog and Rex suspected something.

'Let me at him, please,' said Rex, tugging forward against his lead again and growling in a deep bass note.

'What's with him?' asked the chief inspector. 'I think, Mr Smith, that you should take your dog back outside.'

'I have to get to the competition,' whimpered Alan, trying to get up as well, but falling back with his hands holding his abdomen. 'It should be entering the final rounds soon and I've missed some of the heats!'

Albert exchanged a glance with his son and drew in a deep, thoughtful breath as his mind swirled. The truth of it all. He had a few missing pieces still to identify, but the picture was almost complete. The competition would draw to a close soon, and with it his chance to solve the mystery. With a nod, he tugged Rex back and said, 'Chief Inspector, I believe we should let these two men get back to the competition, don't you? That is if you are up to it, Alan?'

All eyes swung to take in the event organiser, still holding his gut and looking in pain. Using the officers either side of him for support, he struggled back to his feet. 'I feel I must. So much has gone into this event, so many people entered the competition that I cannot let one man spoil it all. The people of York deserve to toast their winner.'

'That's the spirit,' cheered Albert.

Alan's attitude got a, 'Here, here,' from Gary and other noises of encouragement from the other police officers.

CI Doyle said, 'Hendrix, Wilshaw, go with Mr Crystal. Escort both these gentlemen back to the venue and make sure nothing else befalls them.' Then, to Alan and Lee, he said 'I shall need a statement from each of you. A man has died here, and I need to be sure about the circumstances. These officers will remain close by. Please do not attempt to leave the venue until I confirm you are free to do so.'

They both confirmed their understanding, but Albert was already leaving them behind. He had to get back to the museum. He didn't need to see the poster by the giant pudding anymore, he already knew he was right about that part of the mystery: going to the museum would just confirm it.

Eavesdropping

Albert pushed through the flap and back into the marquee. Alan wasn't far behind him now though the man was moving slower than normal due to the damage his gut recently sustained.

Rex was unhappy about leaving the guilty human behind and kept turning his head to look at him. 'Are we not supposed to be doing something about him?' The loud bark made his human look his way. 'Are you listening?' he asked. 'I know your nose doesn't work so there's no point in me asking if you can smell straight, but the two men back there are the same two men that were in the alleyway together yesterday. You had me chase one to save the other. Remember that?' His human was listening intently, so he continued. 'Well, I don't think I was really saving one from the other. I think there's something going on. Also, I think the one who smells of the moped killed the human last night. What I don't understand is how I'm the only one that can smell it.' Complaint delivered, Rex waited for his human to respond.

Albert stared down at his dog, lips pursed as he attempted to decipher the odd noises Rex made. 'Was that all to do with food?' he hazarded. They had just come back into the marquee which was filled with glorious baking smells. It was enough to make Albert hungry so goodness knows what it might be doing to the dog. Rex was always ready to eat so this should be no exception, and it was hours since breakfast. 'You can't have any more Yorkshire pudding, Rex, you'll burst. Now come on. I think that lad who just 'saved' Alan might also be the one who tried to mug him yesterday. I don't suppose that makes any sense to you, but I'll try to explain it shortly.'

Rex couldn't believe his ears. 'That's what I just said!'

'Come along, dog. I need to check on something.' Albert gave his lead another tug, Rex trailing along by his human's side despite feeling like he wanted to lift his leg on his trousers.

'Albert.'

Albert heard Rosie's hopeful call and felt his heart sink a little. He was supposed to be going back to her with a muffin pan. Halfway through her lesson on making her granny's perfect Yorkshire puddings he abandoned her and hadn't been back.

Turning her way, as she fought through the crowd with Teddy balanced on her hip, he grabbed his wallet. 'Rosie, I'm so sorry,' he apologised as soon as she was within conversation distance. 'I'm all caught up in ... something else that's happening here. Can you buy a muffin pan for me?' He offered her a twenty pound note. 'I will come back and find you again shortly. Is that okay?'

'Um, sure,' she replied. 'If you are too busy, don't worry.'

'No, no. I really want to see these perfect Yorkshire puddings and learn how to do it for myself. It's genuinely what I came to York for. I just need to deal with one thing ...'

Rosie said, 'Sure,' again, taking the offered note and agreeing to wait for Albert back in the world record food prep area.

Muttering to himself for his swiss-cheese brain, Albert set off with Rex once more. 'To the museum, boy. We need to look at a photograph.'

The delay in meeting Rosie had, however, allowed Alan, the two officers, and Lee Oliver to catch up. They were at the stage now where trouble still brewed. Pausing to listen, Albert saw Ethan Bentley coming their way.

'Mr Crystal, I really must protest,' the millionaire complained. 'There is something very off about this competition. There have been far too many complaints of fixing going on. I swear some of the contestants knew in advance that they were going to win. Where have you been anyway?'

'Mr Crystal was attacked,' announced PC Hendrix, her voice quiet, but not so softly spoken that Albert couldn't hear her.

Ethan Bentley reacted with stunned shock as one might expect. 'Attacked! Goodness, where? Why? Who was it?'

Alan did his best to look hurt, managing to convey that he was putting a brave face on for the sake of the competition. 'The police believe the man to be a local hoodlum. He was after the prize money, Mr Bentley.'

'Are you alright?' Ethan asked. 'That's the most important thing.'

Alan nodded, placing a hand on Ethan Bentley's shoulder in thanks for his concern. 'I can see this through.'

'But what do we do about the competition. I cannot ... I will not endorse a winner if they have cheated their way to the prize. There will have to be an investigation after the fact, but no winner can be announced today.'

Alan leaned in to speak quietly but reached out with his left hand to bring Lee Oliver closer. Albert struggled to hear what was being said, straining his ears to pick up enough of the words to make sense of it.

It didn't confirm anything for Albert, but it met the criteria for what he believed was happening perfectly. Knowing he had but a few minutes, he got his feet moving again, clicking his mouth at Rex. 'Let's go, boy. This is almost done.'

The Winner

In the museum, Albert found the photograph he wanted. It was hung on the wall at head height with the names listed beneath. The proud faces stood in front of an enormous Yorkshire pudding on a sunny day, each of them smiling at the photographer and forever captured in their glory. Except their glory was about to be overshadowed by a new record and the photograph would be replaced by a new one. He hadn't spotted it when he first saw the picture, but right at the front, just left of centre, a small boy held his mother's hand and smiled for the camera like everyone else. The boy wasn't named as part of the record-breaking team, but the mother was, and that was all Albert needed to confirm what he already believed.

With a sigh, he patted Rex's head where the dog sat on his haunches obediently waiting for his human to finish whatever he was doing.

Arriving back in the marquee, Albert could see all the way down to the stage located in the middle of the tee. It was as he expected: the hub of activity for everything about to happen. Ethan Bentley was hovering at the back of the stage with Alan Crystal and a woman Albert assumed was the third judge. He knew nothing about her other than her name was Amber, and she was a local, but apparently nationally known, food critic and writer.

At the left of the stage, assistants were erecting a pair of tables. Albert could see a line up of bakers all queuing at the left side of the stage as he faced it. Each was carrying a platter of their freshly baked Yorkshire puddings for the final showdown. They would, he guessed, be invited to place their offering down and then wait behind it while the judges sampled and marked their puddings. It was a lot like a baking show he'd once seen on television. His wife, Petunia, God rest her soul, had watched it every week and commented on technique and the complexity of the dishes. Albert sat in his chair and read because the program held little interest, but he looked up every now and then when Petunia said something, just so he could agree with her and pretend to be paying attention.

By the time Albert made it to the vicinity of the stage, the platters of Yorkshire puddings were laid out – ten of them from the ten heats, and the contestants were standing behind them as expected. They all looked eager, all except one pair, a father and son, who looked relaxed by comparison to their peers.

Albert knew why.

He spotted Rosie and waved, getting her attention. Gamely, the young woman raised Teddy's hand and made him wave back. Albert indicated that he would be over once the prize-giving was complete. Rosie, standing just off the stage to the right-hand side lifted her other hand to show a brand-new muffin tin.

Looking about, Albert also spotted Gary, his tall son easy to spot among the crowd of people watching the stage. Gary, seeing his father, started to weave through the crowd to join him.

The compere had been dazzling the audience with his wit again, making Yorkshire pudding jokes and being generally self-deprecating about his figure and how many he'd consumed in his life. Just as he began to wrap up and make ready to hand over to the event organiser, Albert patted Rex's head.

'Are you ready, boy?' he asked.

Rex tilted his head, looking up at his human. Quite prepared to answer that he was ready, he wasn't sure what it was his human needed him to be ready for.

'Ladies and gentlemen,' Alan Crystal's voice rang out loud and clear. 'Welcome to the most important part of today's proceedings: the Yorkshire pudding baking championship. As you all know, this year's winner gets a cash prize of ten thousand pounds.' The crowd gave an oooh and applauded. 'They also get to discuss with Ethan Bentley, founder and CEO of Bentley Brothers supermarkets the chance to provide their Yorkshire puddings to every supermarket in the chain,' he roared with excitement, getting a whoop from the crowd this time along with more applause. 'Truly a prize worth winning, judging this year has been tighter than ever with more contestants than any year previous.'

'It's a fix, I tell thee!' cried Mr Rose from the crowd again.

Smiling, Alan gave a sad nod in Mr Rose's direction. 'There have been many disappointed losers this year.' His comment got a ripple of laughter as event security converged on Mr Rose again. Alan waited for the noise from the audience to peter out before continuing. 'However, the judges were unanimous in their decision to award the contract at Bentley Brothers, and the cheque to ...' he paused for effect, baiting the crowd the way Albert had seen television hosts do.

Albert looked down at Rex, then across at Gary, still making his way through the crowd. He felt something akin to butterflies in his stomach, but it was a case of do it now or miss the chance. Drawing in a deep breath, he shouted, 'Oliver's Bakery from Wetherby!'

His voice filled the silence of the marquee and turned everyone's attention his way. Those standing closest to the old man stepped away, trying to make a little distance between them lest others think they might be together. In less than a second, Albert had a circle of space around his body.

Somewhat taken aback, Alan Crystal looked down at the old man, now easy to spot standing all by himself. His thunder had been stolen, and it took him a moment to recover. 'Why, yes, actually.' A huge smile appeared on Alan's face as he looked out at the audience and said, 'Your winners: Oliver's Bakery of Wetherby!'

Lee Oliver and his father were embracing each other and then they were punching their fists in the air and all around the marquee, people were clapping.

How did you know they were going to win?' asked Gary, finally arriving at his father's side.

Albert didn't answer. Instead, he raised his voice again. 'How much were the bribes, Alan?'

Alan stiffened, but refused to face his accuser. He was shaking hands with Mr Oliver and his son, Lee, and inviting them to the front of the stage.

'You engineered the whole thing, didn't you, Alan? Taking over the event from Brian Pumphrey so you could rig the contest. You needed a big chunk of cash to pay off your gambling debts, isn't that right, Alan?' Albert continued, his voice loud enough to carry over the applause still ringing out.

Event security were rushing to intervene, but as they broke through the crowd of people, they were faced with Gary and his police identification. 'Go away,' Gary insisted.

'What is this?' asked Ethan Bentley. His question was aimed at Alan Crystal, yet it was loud enough that Albert heard.

Albert spoke directly to him, 'The truth, Mr Bentley. Three people have died, and the police have been led on a merry dance so that Alan could get himself out of debt and get the loan shark's enforcer off his back.'

'I have no idea what he is talking about,' snapped Alan, glaring at Albert. 'This is all utter nonsense.'

'Three deaths?' Ethan Bentley repeated. 'Alan, what do you know about this?'

'Don't hand over that cheque, Mr Bentley,' warned Albert as two helpers brought out one of those giant-sized cheques for him to be photographed with.

'It is done!' screamed Alan. 'The winner is announced already!' His face had become bright red. 'The judges' ruling is final and cannot be rescinded.'

Ethan argued, 'I think it probably can if there is any cheating going on.'

'It's a fix, I tell thee!' roared Mr Rose yet again, free to speak his mind now the event security guys were trying to deal with Albert.

'Aye, it is,' shouted Mr Nelson. 'That Alan Crystal guaranteed me a place in the final line up. I had to pay him two grand for that. Two grand!' It was tantamount to admitting he willingly tried to cheat his way through the contest, but incensed at having been ripped off, Mr Nelson was happy to admit his own crime to catch the man behind it.

The audience, thinking the show to be over with the announcement of the winner, were now loving the street theatre occurring around them. Their heads were swinging back and forth as each new person spoke.

On the stage, Alan's head looked ready to explode.

'It gets worse,' Albert shouted. He was guessing the next bit based purely on Rex. 'A man was murdered here late last night, the second man to meet his doom in the space of just a few hours. I feel it necessary to alert you to this, Mr Bentley, because you are currently shaking the murderer's hand.'

The crowd gave a shocked gasp as if cued to do so like a live television audience. Ethan Bentley looked down at his hand and back up at the man holding it. Lee Oliver was as white as a sheet. Hendrix and Wilshaw, as if sensing that he was about to bolt, had climbed onto the stage from their viewing position out of the way at the back.

They were not fast enough though. Not even nearly. Lee Oliver whipped his hand upward, striking the supermarket boss in the face. It wasn't a hard blow and was intended only to get the man out of his way. It caught Ethan by surprise, causing him to leap backward away from the source of violence as Lee Oliver went from stationary to sprinting flat out.

He tore across the stage, heading away from the cops and everyone else.

Seeing him go, Rex bounced onto his paws, suddenly understanding what it was his human wanted him to be ready for.

With an ironic smile, and without taking his eyes from Alan Crystal's, Albert unclipped Rex's lead and said, 'Sic 'em, boy.'

Rex exploded into action. The human had a ten-yard lead but that was nothing. It was their third game of chase and bite and this time Rex wasn't going to lose.

There were cries of alarm when the giant dog ran through the crowd of onlookers. He wanted to put his head down and go but having to negotiate his way through the press of human legs slowed him down. Lee

Oliver leapt from the stage through a gap between people; they'd seen him coming, heard the comment about being a murderer, and chosen to get out of his way. Besides, he was being pursued by a dog the size of a bear.

Left alone on the stage, Alan Crystal couldn't believe what had happened. How did the old man know any of this? He saw Lee run and jump, making good his bid for escape and found his own legs trying to do the same. The two young police officers had chased Lee, leaving him unguarded, which gave him a chance. He was forty years older and significantly slower than the other man, but he ran for the edge of the stage, hopelessly trying to escape the thousands of people around him.

'Grab him!' yelled Gary, starting to clamber onto the stage to give chase. There was no one between Alan and the edge of the marquee. Lee Oliver had made a gap in the crowd, which Alan was now heading for. Evading the law might be improbable, but if someone didn't stop him now, he might escape the venue and then who knew how long he might evade capture.

At the edge of the stage, Alan leapt, roaring like a madman to frighten the people who had already backed away to give him space. However, as he landed and made to run for the exit, a muffin tin swept through the air, colliding with his face with enough force to stop his head even though the rest of his body attempted to keep moving.

Momentum caused his body to flip, Alan Crystal performing an almost perfect somersault. Almost perfect because he failed to land it, hitting the floor with his face instead of his feet.

Stepping out to stand over him, Rosie held the muffin tin aloft in both hands, her injured fingers sticking out at an awkward angle where they were taped together.

Satisfied that he was down for the count, she tucked the muffin tin under her right arm and gratefully accepted Teddy from a man holding the baby and looking very confused about it.

On the stage still, Mr Oliver was looking about in every direction, his panic-stricken eyes darting all over. Seeing that he no longer needed to pursue Alan, Gary dealt with Mr Oliver instead, arresting him in front of the television cameras and event audience.

Rex ran at the canvas of the marquee, smashing it open with his head seconds after his target went through it. There wasn't time to consult his nose for a direction, this was going to have to be done with his eyes.

To find the man, he had to slow down which allowed Lee Oliver to get farther away. Not far enough, of course, not for a creature who could run five times faster than the target he pursued. Spotting him once more, he set off, barking his threats madly and reminding himself to enjoy the pursuit. It would be over soon and who knows when he might next get the chance to chase a truly bad human.

Lee Oliver was in full flight mode, terrified of what might happen if the police caught him. The old man seemed to know everything, how he could didn't matter now, all he could focus on was getting away. The dog was going to catch him for sure this time; there was no ladder to descend to safety, but as that thought flashed across his mind, so he saw the escape route he needed. He didn't dare look back; he knew the dog wasn't far behind because the barking was so loud. He didn't need much of a lead though, jinking to change his direction.

The firefighters were due to be packing up soon. The Yorkshire pudding was baked, the giant monstrosity cooling swiftly now that the fires were out. They'd been on hand as a PR stunt more than for safety, and now they were entertaining some kids and putting on a show; some of the guys showing off because there were pretty girls around.

Station Officer Hamilton didn't see Rex or Lee Oliver approaching. He was at the front of the fire truck explaining to his small audience what the fire truck could do with his firefighters hamming it up to act the parts he described.

Lee Oliver leapt onto the back of the fire truck, swinging a wild punch to knock the first firefighter out of the way. The bemused looks turn to shouts of alarm as the crack of his punch rocked the firefighter's head back and threw him from the rig.

Another firefighter, who was on top of the fire truck, heard the onlookers' gasp and went to see what might have caused it. The ladder was up, the firefighters demonstrating what their truck could do and how far the ladder would reach. It was pointing over toward the museum, extending over the top of the marquee and stretching to reach the museum's roof.

Rex couldn't follow the human up the side of the fire truck, his paws didn't work like that. Angry at being defeated again, he barked and snapped at the human's heels before going around to the far side to see if there was any way to follow. There he discovered the small stage used for the world record photographs where it had been moved out of the way and was tucked close to the fire truck. Leaping first to that, and then scrambling up the side of the truck itself, he came to the ladder bay.

The firefighter had squared off to the human Rex was chasing, but when the human produced a wicked looking knife, the firefighter backed away.

Rex came alongside the retreating human: he wasn't backing away; he wasn't going anywhere.

Full to the brim with fight or flight adrenalin, Lee Oliver could see only one way out and that was up. The ladder would take him up onto the museum roof and from there he could run to adjoining buildings, scaling the rooftops until he could descend and escape. It wasn't just the dog after him though, the police were after him too. The redhead, who until now he thought was cute, and her partner, Wilshaw were arriving at a sprint and would also be on the fire truck soon.

They stopped on the ground as he started to climb, calling for him to give himself up. He preferred his chances of escape, but he would have to be quick before they coordinated more units and officers to the area.

The dog advanced some more, a deep and vicious growl emanating from his chest as he came closer.

'Oh, yeah, doggy? You want some of this?' He pointed the knife in Rex's direction. 'I beat you with a ladder yesterday, you daft mutt,' Lee sneered. 'I guess I'll just do the same again.'

The ladder had to be over a hundred-foot-long at full extent and was inclined upward at a forty-five-degree angle. For Lee, scaling it presented no obstacle at all. Sure in the knowledge that he was going to make it to the museum's roof, he all but ran up it.

Station Officer Hamilton has been caught napping by the sudden change of events. In the pace of five seconds, his crew had gone from entertaining a crowd to having a knife-wielding criminal attacking them and climbing the ladder.

PC Sophie Hendrix had spotted the fire chief and was grabbing his arm already. 'Can you bring the ladder back down?' she shouted urgently. But then her jaw dropped open. 'Oh, my God. What is the dog doing?'

Rex wasn't entirely happy about going up the ladder, but he sure wasn't going to let the human get away for a third time. He started slowly, his front paws finding a balance point on the lower rungs. Angrily, he told his back legs to stop shaking with fear, and pressed on, pursuing his target to a chorus of oohs and aahs from the crowd.

Lee Oliver swung his head around to see what might be causing the crowd's excitement and almost lost his eyes when they bugged right out of his head.

The dog was following him!

'Yeah, puny human!' Rex barked triumphantly seeing the human's fear. 'That's right, dogs can climb ladders. Just not vertical ones.'

'I'm not going to lower it,' yelled the lead firefighter, leaping into action. 'The rungs passing each other might trap their hands or feet. I'm going to swing it around away from the roof!'

It took Albert more than a minute to get outside to see where Rex had gone. Gary was inside arresting Alan Crystal, and everyone wanted to know what the heck was going on because only Albert seemed to have a clue. However, he wasn't answering any questions while Rex was out there chasing a man he believed to be a murderer.

What he saw, when he made it through the press of other people all keen to see what was happening outside, stole his breath away.

Rex was halfway along a fire ladder, forty feet in the air and climbing with Lee Oliver brandishing a knife in his face. As Albert watched, the ladder was swinging around, away from the marquee but a fall from that height would kill Rex no matter where he landed and Albert struggled to find a breath as he watched the aerial standoff advance toward a terrible conclusion.

Lee Oliver couldn't believe it when the ladder started moving. That they might slew it away from the museum roof had not occurred to him and now he was stuck between the angry looking dog with his rows of nasty teeth and a fall to certain injury.

He had to get rid of the dog and get back down to the fire truck. His priority to escape had switched – now he was trying to stay alive as the ground looked a long way down from his current height. The dog wouldn't stop advancing though. It was slow, checking each paw before he put the next one down, but the gap, which had been thirty feet, was now more like ten and Lee didn't want to go any higher up the ladder.

He swore at the dog, uselessly hoping it might convince him to go back down. Then he tried shaking the ladder, gripping tightly with his hands, something he knew the dog couldn't do, he threw himself around. Side to side and then up and down, attempting to shake the dog loose.

It almost worked.

Rex hunkered down to the ladder when it started to move. Biting a rung to anchor himself a little better and hooking his front paws around a rung as best he could, he held on until the human gave up. Then he started forward again.

Back on the ground next to the fire truck, Hendrix and Wilshaw were joined by Chief Inspector Doyle who heard the ruckus and sent his constable to see what was going on. The answer made him run to see for himself.

'Mr Smith,' he addressed Albert, picking him from the crowd just as he sent Jones and Washington to relieve Gary and cuff both Alan Crystal and Mr Oliver senior. 'I thought Mr Oliver was the hero who saved Mr Crystal.' It was posed as a statement but sounded like a question, CI Doyle voicing openly how confused he was by the turn of events.

Gary came to stand beside his father. A little out of breath, he said, 'Well that was invigorating. I haven't physically arrested anyone myself in years.'

Chief Inspector Doyle acknowledged his superior's efforts with a nod. 'I find myself at something of a loss,' he admitted with a trace of irritation showing. 'Would either of you be so kind as to tell me what is going on.'

Albert didn't take his eyes off the ladder. 'Just as soon as my dog is safe,' he replied. Albert's heart was beating at twice its usual pace, which he doubted was good for him. If Rex fell, he wondered if it might just stop.

On the ladder, Rex advanced again, creeping forward another rung. He was too high off the ground and refusing to look down because he knew it would make him feel ill. The target was ahead, that was all that mattered, so he focussed on that and went up yet another rung.

Lee Oliver couldn't shake the dog loose and could see the gathering crowd surrounding the fire truck. Filled with rage that he had been caught just when he was onto the biggest score of his life, he wanted to lash out and hurt something. He wouldn't win any points killing the dog in front of an audience, but he didn't care. The old man fingered him as Jordan's killer so he was going to jail for life anyway. Killing the dog might give him some satisfaction.

He'd have to do it quickly though, they were lowering the ladder now, dropping the angle rather than retracting it and soon he would be low enough to jump.

The dog came closer – five feet, then three, and Lee readied himself. He was going to kick the dog, let it bite his boot and swing the knife. The dog might think itself to be tough, but he was about to change that.

Rex could see the human had stopped moving, and he knew the ladder was going down. He felt good about that, but if he didn't get the job done soon, the ladder would be low enough for the human to swing underneath it and jump. Rex didn't think the target would get far, the other humans would tackle him, but he wanted to win the chase and bite game and he was so close now.

The target had the knife in his right hand, Rex could see it, and understood the danger it represented. Pushing fear to one side, he lunged.

The human kicked out, and Rex caught the kick with his teeth.

Lee Oliver took the pain of his foot being crushed inside his boot with a scream, but as he swung his body forward, scything his knife toward the dog with cries of horror from the audience below, he felt his whole leg yank forward. The dog had just walked himself backward off the side of the ladder!

Rex smiled at the human. 'Got you.' Then he closed his eyes and let gravity take him.

The Big Reveal

They say time can stand still in a moment of terror, and for Albert that proved to be true. The ladder had been slewed around so it was hanging over the other side of the fire truck. Many in the crowd had chosen to follow the ladder as it swung around and got to see the dog fall. The man on the ladder had let go with both hands to swing his knife so when the dog went, biting tightly to the human's foot, the man went too.

Albert didn't see them hit the ground, a mercy he was grateful for, but when the screams of horror turned to guffaws of laughter, his breath caught, and his heart started beating again. Holding onto Gary to keep himself upright when Rex fell, he pushed off now and tottered toward the fire truck and beyond as fast as he could go.

'What the heck are they laughing at?' he asked aloud, hoping that some miracle had befallen his dog.

When he got around the obstacles and Chief Inspector Doyle and his officers cleared a path through, he stood and laughed as well. He laughed so much he thought he might wet himself.

Rex was standing chest deep in the world's largest Yorkshire pudding and attempting to eat his way out. He couldn't have looked happier if he had two tails to wag. The fluffy moist pudding beneath the crispy top had cushioned his fall, apparently saving him from injury while providing a nourishing reward for his efforts.

Quite how the dog had known the pudding would break his fall or if he even did, would remain a mystery forever, but as the laughter continued, a confused, pudding covered form erupted from the surface a few feet from Rex. His knife had been lost in the fall, but Lee Oliver was still madder than a hornet in a jam jar.

'In you go then,' said Chief Inspector Doyle, nodding his head at his officers.

An amused chorus of, 'Yes, sirs,' came back as the four plain clothes officers jumped over the side of the giant, still-warm pan and began to wade across. In seconds Lee Oliver was cuffed and being dragged away.

Albert continued to coax Rex to the edge of the pan, but the dog was refusing to budge.

From the crowd of onlookers, someone shouted, 'It must taste pretty good.'

To which someone else shouted, 'I'm going to try it.'

In seconds, hands were grabbing chunks of the swimming pool sized Yorkshire pudding and stuffing their faces with it.

Then the food fight broke out.

Afterwards, when a lucky photographer caught picture after picture of ordinary folks engaged in a slapstick movie event, no one would agree who had started it. So far as Albert was concerned, Rex was the guilty party, but he wasn't holding it against the dog. Rex had been a real champion.

The fire fighters, also guilty of joining in, had to use the hose, at CI Doyle's request, to stop the fun before someone got hurt. In the aftermath, when the pudding looked like tons of muck and little else, Albert found himself surrounded by people wanting an explanation.

The chief inspector was among them. 'Mr Smith, I now have to sort all this mess out. I have two men in custody, both arrested in connection with the murders of Brian Pumphrey and Jordan Banks. I have three bodies, now that Warren Bradley is on his way to the morgue, and I have

201

another man in custody, Reginald 'Beefy' Botham. Doubtless, you will claim he is innocent and I'm afraid I am not letting you go anywhere until I have wrung from you every piece of information you claim to have because, quite frankly, I don't have any evidence against either of the suspects.'

Albert avoided most of the food fight by walking quickly away from it just before it started, but he still had a smear of Yorkshire pudding grease on his scalp where a loose piece struck the back of his head before he could get far enough away. The sun was beginning to set behind him, and at the end of his lead Rex lay contentedly on the floor, his sides fit to burst with Yorkshire pudding.

Albert wanted to go back to his bed and breakfast and get the bath he'd promised himself more than twenty-four hours ago, but the people looking at him now deserved an explanation.

Because he was yet to say anything and several seconds had ticked by, Gary stepped in to usher everyone else back. 'Okay, folks, let's give the old man some breathing space, eh?' he was the ranking police officer on the scene, even if it wasn't his city, but Albert spoke up before anyone moved away.

'I could do with a cup of tea,' he said. 'My joints are a bit weary too, but if you find me a chair and hot mug of char, I promise to do my best to explain what I think I know.'

No one could argue with his requests, simple as they were, the entourage around the old man and his dog all moving as one toward the marquee.

The event was over, the crowds of visitors gone. Stallholders were packing up, so too the bakers, but the competitors, all there vying for the cash prize and more coveted offer of a contract with Bentley Brothers, were still there and they were arguing.

'So who wins?' one woman demanded to know. She, like many others, was haranguing poor Sarah. With Brian dead and Alan in custody, the management of the competition, indeed of the whole event, was in disarray. Albert wanted no part of it, and as he wearily lowered himself into a chair when Gary brought him one, he felt glad he could ignore it.

Chief Inspector Doyle was urging PC Hendrix to hurry up with the tea and arguing with her about a question she raised about workplace misogyny since she was the only woman there and the one expected to fetch the drinks.

Both the Olivers and Alan Crystal, a piece of gauze covering his nose where Rosie broke it, were in cuffs and being held by the three male plain-clothes police officers, CI Doyle pointed out, not that his argument had much impact on the self-righteous, and probably correct, woman.

Waiting for the kettle to boil, Albert organised his thoughts and like a schoolteacher at story time, found himself surrounded by expectant faces when he began to talk.

'You all know that the museum had suffered several break ins,' he started. 'Things have been stolen but what kind of thief would steal from a museum dedicated to a regional dish? What could there be of value for the thief to then sell on? I leave you to ponder that for a moment.' Albert sipped his tea. It was just right.

'The double murders, Mr Smith,' CI Doyle prompted with pleading in his voice. 'I'll give you a pass on Warren Bradley since we know what happened to him, but please tell me why the morgue is filling up.'

Albert set the steaming mug down again. 'Yes. Well, for a start, you are wrong that you know what happened to Warren Bradley, and there was only one murder.' His statement got a round of questioning looks. 'You see,' he continued before anyone could interrupt him, 'Brian Pumphrey was very much against the world record attempt. Gary and I were witness to his attitude on the matter ourselves, so too the bakers hired by the event organiser. Alan Crystal will testify to the same. Brian even tried to stop it from going ahead yesterday when the ingredients were found to have been tampered with.'

'Yes, Mr Smith,' said the chief inspector. 'That is when my detectives arrested Mr Botham. He openly threatened to kill Brian Pumphrey with a dozen witnesses and then made sure there was no one around when the murder occurred. How is it that this is not a murder?' CI Doyle was challenging the old man, but not in a negative way - his tone was open and curious.

Albert took another sip of his tea. 'In the museum there is a photograph on the wall of the previous world record. It was set in 1987 by a team from Uncle Bert's. Endorsed by the company, volunteers at their factory baked a crisp, golden, and above all giant Yorkshire pudding. Pictured in the photograph and holding his mother's hand, is the eight-year-old Brian Pumphrey.' His revelation made eyes bug. 'I didn't see it at first. It was only when they put a poster sized version up that I noticed the little boy and his resemblance to the man who so tragically lost his life yesterday while trying to ruin the world record attempt.'

'How can you be sure that's what he was doing?' asked PC Hendrix.

Albert offered her a wry smile. 'I can't. That's your job. I believe though that you will swiftly find the evidence you require. Brian kept calling the record attempt pointless and claiming that no one cared about it. He was lying though because he cared about it more deeply than anyone else. He cared enough to try to ruin it because he wanted the previous record to stand.'

Gary nodded. 'That's right. I heard him say it.'

Albert continued. 'The flour had been cut with salt before or after delivery. I suspect it was after but whatever the case, someone on the event committee must have placed the order for the ingredients and I'm willing to bet it was Brian. He wanted the attempt to fail so his mother's legacy would live on, but that wasn't enough. You see, Alan Crystal manoeuvred himself to gain control of an event which Brian had run for more than a decade. Didn't you, Alan?'

Alan Crystal refused to answer.

Albert continued regardless. 'Brian thought of the World Yorkshire Pudding Championships as his event, and what Alan was doing to add all the glitter and glamour was too much for him to take. He was trying to scupper the record attempt but when his tampered ingredients were discovered, he knew it wouldn't be long before someone tried to find out how it happened, and the trail would lead back to him. That's why he cut a button from the cuff of Alan's rather fancy jacket and planted it in the bakers' container.

'He did what?' blurted Alan, trying to twist his head and body so he could see his cuffs. Washington, already gripping Alan's right bicep tightly, gave him a shake to stop him from moving.

Albert carried on. 'There would be no good reason for Alan to have ever gone in there and the button was so unique there couldn't possibly be two jackets around with the same one.'

Chief Inspector Doyle saw the connection. 'The threads on the carpet in his office.'

'And the scissors on the desk,' Albert reminded him. 'When you check, I believe you will find Brian's fingerprints on them. Hardly damning I know.'

'Did Brian poison Alan?' Gary asked, his head tilted to one side as he tried to see the mystery from a different angle.

The chief inspector and the other officers didn't know what he was referring to, which prompted an explanation where Gary told them about Alan's bout of projectile vomiting the previous evening.

Albert shook his head. 'I thought that might be the case too. Rex knocked Brian over, and when we got him back to his feet, he had a dark stain down his front which we all thought was blood.'

'That's right,' said Gary, unsure where his father was going with this.

'He told us it was cough medicine, didn't he?' Albert prompted his son.

Gary obediently replied, 'Yes.'

With his right hand, Albert reached down to pet Rex, patting the dog's head and scratching his ears. 'Rex found it somewhere and brought it to me.' Albert left out the part where he believed Rex knew it was an important clue because his audience didn't need to hear that. 'It wasn't cough medicine at all. The bottle was a prescription for his cat, Fluffikins.' From his pocket, Albert produced the bottle. 'It's something called, Syrup of Ipecac which is used to induce vomiting. If you remember, Alan got some on his hand when he helped Brian up. My guess is he accidentally then wiped his hand on his mouth or something. It was most likely a mild dose he got, yet enough to produce the result Gary and I witnessed.'

Alan groaned. 'I did it to myself? I can't believe it.'

Chief Inspector Doyle's face could not be more creased from frowning if he tried. 'Mr Smith, you are yet to tell me why you think Brian Pumphrey's death was not murder.'

Albert nodded to concede the point and took another swig of his tea. 'Mr Botham didn't shove Brian into the mixer and he didn't see it because he wasn't in the marquee.'

'Yes, he was, Dad,' argued Gary. 'He sent everyone else outside to get fresh ingredients.'

'And he's yet to provide anything close to an alibi for where he was when Brian went into the mixing machine,' added CI Doyle.

'That's because he cannot,' Albert told them with an annoying grin. He was enjoying this but doing so at the expense of everyone else. 'Beefy is having an affair with Suzalls.'

The chief inspector threw his arms in the air. 'Who the heck is Suzalls?'

'Susan Parker,' Albert supplied. 'The wife of Dave 1 and another member of the baking team hired by Alan Crystal.'

'Dave Won?' questioned CI Doyle, not sure he heard right.

Rather than explain about the three Daves, Albert begged, 'Just believe me on this. Beefy is having an affair with another man's wife and he was … canoodling with her when Brian Pumphrey had his accident.'

PC Hendrix's face was pinched with misunderstanding. 'Canoodling?'

'Um … smooching?' Albert tried a different word, wondering if canoodling was another of those terms which had been dropped by the generations that followed his.

'They were getting it on,' supplied Wilshaw, with accompanying inappropriate actions which did, at least, deal with any remaining ambiguity.

CI Doyle clicked his fingers, stifling Wilshaw's amusement instantly. 'Wilshaw get on the radio and get Susan Parker and this Dave character picked up for questioning. I want this story corroborated.'

'Beefy Botham was otherwise engaged and away from the mixing machines. Whether Brian had been waiting for his chance or just happened along at that time and took advantage of the machines being unguarded we shall never know. However, I feel certain he intended to have another attempt at scuppering the world record attempt. You see the finished product has to be edible, so there must have been hundreds of different things he could add to the batter to make it taste terrible.'

'That's what the aniseed smell was!' blurted Gary, snapping his fingers. 'He was adding it to the mix, and he fell in!'

Acting fast, the chief inspector looked at his constable. 'Ferris get on the radio and find out if the pathologists have the batter they took off of Brian Pumphrey yet. I want to know if it contains high levels of aniseed and if they found a container. If he fell in, whatever he had the additive in, must have gone in with him.'

Ferris stepped away, using his radio to speak with someone as Albert continued. 'The machine would have been on, and Brian would not have wanted to draw attention to himself by switching it off. Maybe he caught his cuff on the mechanism and was pulled in. Perhaps he leaned too far and overbalanced. Whatever the case, in he went, and there was no way out for him. By the time Brian was found, he'd already suffocated in the batter.'

Everyone was quiet for a time, working the flow of events and motivations through their minds. The silence was broken by Ferris saying, 'The pathologists' office has confirmed a large quantity of aniseed extract in the batter along with a supermarket chain bottle of it, the type home chefs buy.'

Looking directly at Albert, the chief inspector let his shoulders sag slightly. 'Okay, Mr Smith. Let's assume we are down to one murder. I do hope you are not going to claim Jordan Banks accidentally stabbed himself.'

Albert didn't return the chief inspector's wry smile; this wasn't a humorous subject. 'You all heard the claims that the competition was fixed,' Albert was asking them to nod their confirmation.

'I can still hear them arguing about it now,' said Gary, referring to the remaining contestants still pointlessly demanding the competition be rerun or their entries be judged again.

This was the difficult bit and how to adequately explain the multifaceted parts was still troubling Albert. Did he start where his story began – with the mugging? Or should he start where his suspicions arose?

'The thefts from the museum which I asked you to keep in mind, they were all low value items such as photographs, historical documents and early examples of the tins Yorkshire puddings were made in. No thief on the planet would bother stealing them. However, also missing were items of greater value: a computer, a new office printer, and more. The theft of the lower value items was meant to make the police believe a thief had chosen to target the museum when in fact the curator was selling them.' Albert got a lot of surprised or confused looks in response to his allegation. 'On his desk, I found a note. It was hard to decipher but I believe Warren Bradley, who I first saw in the alleyway near the station when Alan Crystal was mugged, was acting as the enforcer for a loan shark.' He swung his attention to the man in question, who was standing between Jones and Washington with his arms cuffed behind his back. 'Was it gambling debt, Alan? Or something else?'

Alan was looking at the floor, and for a moment Albert didn't think he was going to answer. When he mumbled something, CI Doyle insisted he speak up, and Alan shouted for all to hear, 'It was gambling debt! Okay? I love the horses. The damned nags keep beating the odds though.' He sounded grumpy about his run of bad luck, missing the point that he could have just stopped laying bets at any point instead of trying to gamble his way out of trouble.

'The odds,' Albert commented. 'That was what beat you, huh? So you decided to bet on a result you could control.' Addressing his audience, Albert explained. 'Alan Crystal needed money to pay off debts and he got desperate enough that he concocted the whole event around him beating the odds. He decided in advance who was going to win and then set out to make as much money from his prior knowledge as possible. He didn't have any money though and his lenders had lost faith. They wanted their money back, so he agreed to pay them and arranged a meeting with Warren Bradley.'

'The mugging,' Gary concluded.

Albert nodded, watching Lee Oliver's face turn white. 'Yes. Alan was on his way to an arranged meeting but never planned to hand over the money he owed. He stole his own computer and printer, selling them to get some cash, and covering the crime up by stealing artefacts from around the museum.'

A snort of despair escaped Alan's nose. 'How do you know that?'

Albert gave him a level stare. 'Did you throw the things away, or did you have some conscience as the museum curator and merely store them in your house?'

Alan's shoulder sagged, knowing it was too late to bother bluffing or lying now. 'The garage,' he admitted sadly.

'Of course, selling a few items wasn't enough to give him the kind of cash he needed. He took bribes from those contestants he believed would see the benefit of making it through the heats to the final. He could have used that cash to pay off his debt, but then I don't know how far in the hole he was. The note on his desk was confusing at first, until I thought about the accusations of rigging an event. If you knew in advance the outcome of a sporting event you could place a bet on, how much money would you wager?'

He didn't need an answer, the faces around him said it all: they would bet every penny they had and maybe then some more they didn't have.

'Alan couldn't get great odds on the outcome of the competition. It was only on the bookkeepers' radar because Ethan Bentley's people have been hyping it as a marketing strategy to get interest going before the launch of the new product. The odds were short, but what if he tied the outcome to another event? If I have deciphered the note correctly, he got odds of a hundred to one and I think he combined guessing the right winner of the baking competition with the world record being broken. He took two thousand pounds from each of the contestants that agreed to pay it. Let's assume that was all of those in the final. That's twenty thousand, placed on a bet at a hundred to one.'

'That's two million pounds,' whistled Gary. 'Enough motivation for most.'

'It was all set up, and he knew he could get away with it. But the lenders were breathing down his neck so he set up the meeting with their enforcer, Warren Bradley, and got Lee Oliver to help him stage a mugging. He needed the lenders to believe he was genuinely trying to pay them back. Tell me, Alan, did you think they would give you extra time?'

He shrugged. 'I thought they might let me off.' His admission made those listening laugh.

'He hadn't counted on me showing up with Rex. What was it he promised you?' he asked the Olivers. 'First prize in the competition?'

The police officers could tell by the suspects' faces that the old man was right on the money.

Chief Inspector Doyle picked up the story. 'He took bribes to get them into the final but when Warren grabbed him outside, another judge stepped in to award the prizes and gave it to those most deserving, not those who had paid.'

'Hence the complaint from Mr Nelson,' Gary concluded.

'It was going wrong before that,' Albert reminded them. 'Mr Ross knew he was a serious contender but knowing he was going to win, Mr Oliver foolishly rubbed Mr Ross's nose in it, tipping him off that something was amiss.'

'How did you work it out?' asked the chief inspector.

Albert puffed out his lips for a second. 'I think it was when I saw Alan's face when he returned to the event this morning and heard the less than positive report from Dave 2. The bakers were less than confident about the world record attempt and Alan was horrified by the concept that he might have made the wrong bet.'

212

'I would have got nothing,' Alan admitted sadly.

'So who killed Jordan Banks?' Wilshaw wanted to know.

'Lee Oliver did,' Albert stated boldly. 'My guess would be a dispute over money was the cause. In fact, since we are yet to identify the person driving the moped on which Lee Oliver escaped from the fake mugging, I'm willing to bet that is where Jordan comes in.'

Lee Oliver tutted. 'He saw Crystal get taken away in the ambulance yesterday and got upset because he thought he wouldn't get his cut. I didn't mean to hurt him, all right? It was his knife, not mine.'

Albert looked at CI Doyle. 'I think you can take that as a confession.'

Lee swung his head around. 'What? No, I never …'

Chief Inspector Doyle cut him off. 'I think that'll do it.' With a nod to his officers, he said, 'Take them away.' There was some protesting, but there was nothing the three could say that would get them off.

'There's one thing I don't get,' said Wilshaw, pausing everyone just as they were leaving. 'Warren Bradley grabbed Alan Crystal and gave him a beating. How does that fit in with any of this?'

Albert was impressed that someone had picked up on the incongruity. 'It doesn't fit. That wasn't part of Alan's plan. He was almost over the line when Warren grabbed him. I think Lee genuinely saved him from an even worse beating. Is that about right?' he asked the three suspects.

Alan took a moment but nodded his head in a barely perceptible motion.

Albert saw it. 'That was when I knew I had it worked out.' Alan looked up, wanting to hear more. 'You claimed Warren was beating you to get you to give up the cash prize. The same one you lied about being in the briefcase. How was Warren going to get the money?' Albert asked. 'He had you tied up for the beating.'

Alan hung his head, seeing how weak his on-the-spot lie had been.

Chief Inspector Doyle clicked his fingers. 'Get them out of here.'

Now that the police officers had dispersed to take the three suspects to the local police station and corroborate all that Albert claimed, the old man was left alone with Rex and Gary.

'You know, Dad,' Gary said, 'That was really quite something. I don't think I could have ever worked that out for myself.'

Albert hoped that wasn't true, his son had risen through the ranks of the Metropolitan police to be a senior detective after all. To respond, he said, 'I just pieced it together. I think anyone could have done it, had they been in the same places at the same times and have seen the same things.'

Gary knew his father was being modest and was about to say so when he noticed a young woman waiting timidly a few yards away. He couldn't remember her name now that she was out of the baker's uniform that had it embroidered on but recognised her as a woman his father had been talking to. She had a baby balanced on her left hip and a I-don't-want-to-disturb-you look on her face.

'Everything all right?' Gary asked her.

The question drew his father's eyes around to the right. 'Rosie,' he gasped. Yet again he'd forgotten the poor girl.

'I've got your muffin pan and your change,' she said, holding a bag up with her right arm. Her cheeks coloured. 'One of the muffin holes is a bit dented,' she admitted.

Albert chuckled at the memory of Alan's face stopping dead when she hit him with it. 'I shall treasure it all the more,' he told her honestly. 'I never did get to see your Granny's wonderful Yorkshire puddings,' he lamented. Then a lightning bolt of inspiration hit him, propelling him from his chair like he was in his twenties again.

In fact, he got up so fast, he had to take a moment to let his head settle for fear he was about to fall over again. Then he tossed Gary Rex's lead. 'Stay here please, Rosie, I will be right back.'

'But I have to go,' she wailed after him.

He walked backward for a couple of paces. 'No, you don't, Rosie. You need to stay right there. Please indulge me for just a couple of minutes more.' He hurried away, convinced the sweet girl would stay put until he got back and just prayed he could pull off one last miracle for the day.

Outside, he spotted a gleaming black Bentley Continental and knew it had to be the right car. Waving his arms and yelling like a madman did the trick, convincing the driver to stop his car long enough to see what the crazy old man could possibly want.

'Mr Bentley,' Albert wheezed, out of breath from trying to run. 'You still need a perfect Yorkshire pudding recipe, don't you?' It was a question, but Albert wasn't waiting for an answer. 'There's a young woman inside with pudding that will blow your socks off.' Albert used Rosie's own choice of phrase from when she talked about them. He sure hoped it wasn't just hyperbole.

Ethan Bentley was tired and disappointed. The project was an embarrassing bust and a waste of investment. 'Sorry, I'm just not interested. I cannot be sure any of the contestants were not involved in the cheating scandal here and I won't align my name with them.' He made it sound final and was about to buzz his window back up when Albert slammed his hand down on it to stop him.

'She wasn't a contestant, Mr Bentley. She didn't enter with her amazing puddings because she couldn't afford the entry fee. She's a single mum with girl-next-door looks and a hard luck tale to rival most. Her Yorkshire puddings are to die for,' Albert hoped since he hadn't even seen one yet, 'and you will be throwing away a marketing dream come true if you don't come inside and meet her.'

A little more than forty minutes later, which was how long it took to pick Rosie up off the floor and send her to fetch the batter she made hours ago, find an oven and get some oil smoking hot, Rosie produced the tastiest looking Yorkshire puddings Albert had ever laid eyes on.

Ethan Bentley had indulged the old man and the young woman because he thought of himself, above all else, as a man of the people and he didn't want to be seen to be rude. He did little to hide his impatience and desire to leave though. That is until the tray of Yorkshire puddings appeared.

She made a dozen using the muffin pan with the dent in the bottom and tipped them out onto a handy plate Gary found. Then Gary, Albert, and Rosie waited with bated breath to see what the supermarket millionaire would say.

Rex didn't even wag his tail when the tasty-smelling puddings arrived. He wasn't feeling great and had vowed to never touch another Yorkshire pudding so long as he lived.

'They have a good rise,' Ethan remarked objectively. 'And good colour,' he added when no one else spoke. Having scrutinised them visually for long enough, he picked one up and tore it into two pieces. 'Good consistency too,' he commented, pursing his lips and frowning. There really was only one test left. Into his mouth went one half of the Yorkshire pudding, and with three people watching him the self-made millionaire chewed and thought and chewed.

Once he'd swallowed and thought for a few seconds more, he popped the second half into his mouth and repeated the process.

After about another minute of silence, he looked at Rosie. 'How big is your factory?' he asked.

Rosie snorted a laugh. 'I don't even have a job. There is no factory. Just my granny's recipe.'

That gave Ethan something to think about, but after a couple of seconds he said, 'If I built you a factory, how many could you make a day?'

Rosie had never needed to consider such concepts before but faced with the challenge now she shook her head. 'I don't think making these in a factory will work, Mr Bentley.'

Albert's jaw fell open. Ethan Bentley was offering to solve all her money worries. Not just now but forever, and she was telling him it wouldn't work. There's integrity for you, he thought, but he wanted to bonk something off the top of her skull.

Ethan Bentley nodded his head. 'I see.'

However, Rosie wasn't finished. 'I think the mistake the mass-produced Yorkshire pudding people make is in believing they can give people as good a product at home after it has been frozen. Frozen Yorkshire puddings just aren't the same.'

Ethan wasn't following her line of thinking. 'I'm sorry, what are you saying?'

'I think you need to sell batter, Mr Bentley. If you want to give people the high-end Yorkshire pudding experience, you can't just do what other supermarkets are doing but better, you need to rethink the whole thing. Sell the customers a batter kit they can bake themselves at home. That would be innovative and get a better product to the customer.'

Ethan Bentley saw the truth of it and his face lit up like a pinball machine hitting the winning score. Smiling at Rosie while Gary bounced Teddy on his knee, he said, 'Rosie, you are going to make a lot of money.'

There was shaking of hands, and a tear from Rosie who couldn't believe the change of luck. Albert felt good about himself, and Gary was mostly in awe of all his father had achieved.

A few moments later, they got up to leave. The event was over, their time in York almost done, but as Rex got slowly to his feet, he spotted the cat.

Fluffikins was under a table just a couple of yards away from where he hissed at the dog. 'Eat something, mutt? You look like a paperweight.'

Rex considered his options, and his promise to eat the cat if he ever saw him again. He knew it wouldn't do to go back on his threat but feeling like he might willingly take some Syrup of Ipecac, he sniggered at the cat instead, and followed his human back out into the night.

Where Next?

At York train station the next morning Albert and Gary were waiting for his train to arrive. It would zoom south at a surprising speed, delivering Gary back into London almost exactly two hours after setting off.

'Arbroath next, isn't it?' Gary tried to confirm after checking his memory.

'It's supposed to be,' Albert replied. 'I might go to Cumbria instead.'

Gary raised an eyebrow. 'Oh, why's that?'

Albert grimaced, unsure what to admit and what to keep secret. When his kids were growing up, he employed a policy of being honest with them about everything. It had stood him well in life, and he chose to continue following it now. 'There was a break in at the sausage factory a few weeks ago and a man went missing.'

Gary had to frown. 'Wait. There was a break in, and the thieves stole a person?'

Albert rolled his eyes. 'No, dummy. There was a break in, and a load of equipment was stolen. A   person working there just happened to go missing at exactly the same time.

'Soooo, why are you changing your plan and going to Cumbria instead of Arbroath?'

Albert huffed out a breath. 'To see if the two things might actually be connected after all.'

Gary sighed. His father hadn't talked about it for two days and he hoped it might be done with. Apparently not. 'This is that conspiracy thing again, isn't it, Dad.'

'Yes,' Albert replied as neutrally as he could manage because he couldn't work out whether to sigh or snap.

Gary opened his mouth and then closed it again. He had been about to berate his father for his foolish thoughts but then remembered his incredible piece of detective work to figure out all that was happening at the Yorkshire pudding event.

'When I get back to London, I'll look into those things you asked me to,' Albert turned his head to see if his son was teasing and about to make a joke. 'The missing chefs and missing foods. I'll let you know what I turn up. Okay?'

Albert patted his eldest son's arm. 'Thank you, Gary. That means a lot.'

They fell silent for a moment as they watched the London express train pull into the platform. Albert was to be alone for the next part of his trip, but he was fine with that. He wasn't really alone after all because he had Rex for company. Rex was having some digestive issues this morning, due entirely, in Albert's opinion, to the half-ton of Yorkshire pudding the dog ate the previous day. His own train was due in on a different platform in twelve minutes. He had already made his decision to go to Cumberland when he found the news article the previous evening.

Was there something to find there though? Was there really something going on? Or was he just a daft old man imagining a master criminal where none existed. Well, he thought, at the very least, he'd get to eat some really great sausages.

The End

(Except it isn't. Not only are there more books coming, there's more on the next few pages.)

Author's Notes

I wonder how many people living in York will read this book. Those who do, will argue with my use of geography because there is no green stretch on which a marquee could fit in the area I chose to describe. The river is there, but it doesn't sit as far above the water as I chose to suggest. I call it artistic license though I am not sure that is the right term.

Occasionally someone attempts to correct what I have written, forgetting that it is fiction. I could use fictitious places, which would eliminate the issue, but using regional dishes for this series, such as I am, I am happier tying them to real villages, towns, and cities.

York is, by the way, a fabulous place to visit. If, for example, I were talking to an American wanting to come to England, I would recommend York over London, purely for the sights one can see on a walking tour. York city wall is but one of the sights in this beautiful city.

I made the pudding museum up. Honestly, it may actually exist. Only now as I write this author's note has it occurred to me to look it up, and now I won't just because it's too late to change the story.

In contrast to the invented museum, Syrup of Ipecac is real. Whether modern veterinary practices still use it I could not guess, but certainly, it had been employed in the past to make cats vomit and would have the same effect on humans.

It is full autumn in my garden and has rained a vast percentage of the time I have taken to write this novel. I spend a lot of my writing hours in an unheated log cabin at the bottom of my garden. I get to watch the rain beating down, and see the colours change from the lush green of summer, through the autumnal shades of yellow, orange, and brown. Soon the view from my window will be one with few leaves at all in it. To

223

combat that, I planted lots of evergreens, but still the garden will look a little drab soon and for the next few months.

This book took longer than usual to write, interrupted constantly by DIY tasks as I converted our dining room into a playroom for our children. Little Hermione isn't yet six months, so it is very much for Hunter at the moment. He can spread out and we get to reclaim our living room which was slowly being taken over by Brio trains and Hot Wheels cars. I fitted underfloor heating beneath anti-slip ceramic tiles and reworked the wiring and plumbing plus had to decorate the whole thing. Like the book, it took longer than I intended and ended up more complicated than might have been strictly necessary. I also put my back out sawing skirting boards of all things.

I don't think it was the skirting boards that did it. Rather, a combination of spending my time in a sedentary lifestyle and a long history of sports and other injuries which include two prolapsed discs. Hopefully the book makes sense, but I wrote the last thirty percent while stoned on painkillers, so it could either be genius or tripe. At this point, still stoned, I cannot tell.

Albert and Rex, at the time of writing in October 2020, are my best-selling characters and ones I particularly love. My decision to have a near-octogenarian central character was controversial because no one does that.

Why did I? Because that's where I am heading. Yes, I have several decades before I get there, but having met sprightly people in their eighties and nineties, I know how they can be and that's a model I can follow. Albert is a bit cheeky, but still utterly determined to be who he is until time finally stops him. Albert and Rex have a long way to go before their story will be done.

Take Care

Steve Higgs

Roast beef and Yorkshire pudding is recognized across the world as a traditional British dish, but the history of the Yorkshire pudding is shrouded in mystery, and its origins are virtually unknown. There are no cave drawings, hieroglyphics, and so far, no one has unearthed a Roman Yorkshire pudding dish buried beneath the streets of York. The puddings may have been brought to the shores by any of the invading armies across the centuries, but unfortunately, any evidence of this has yet to be discovered.

What has been found, though, are recipes, including one dating back to the early 1700s. Overall, they are similar in the most basic sense, but there are a few interesting differences.

The first recorded Yorkshire pudding recipe appeared in a book called *The Whole Duty of a Woman* in 1737 and was listed as "A Dripping Pudding." The dripping comes from spit-roast meat. The recipe reads: "Make a good batter as for pancakes, put it in a hot toss-pan over the fire with a bit of butter to fry the bottom a little, then put the pan and batter under a shoulder of mutton instead of a dripping pan, frequently shaking it by the handle and it will be light and savoury, and fit to take up when your mutton is enough; then turn it in a dish, and serve it hot."

The next recorded recipe launched the strange pudding from a local delicacy to Britain's favourite dish. It appeared in *The Art of Cookery, Made Plain and Easy* by Hannah Glasse in 1747. Glasse was one of the most famous food writers of the time, and the popularity of her book spread the word of the Yorkshire pudding. "It is an exceedingly good pudding, the gravy of the meat eats well with it," states Glasse. A somewhat different instruction in her recipe is "to set your stew-pan on it under your meat, and let the dripping drop on the pudding, and the heat of the fire come to it, to make it of a fine brown."

Mrs. Beeton may have been Britain's most famous food writer of the 19th century, but her 1866 recipe omitted one of the fundamental rules for making Yorkshire pudding: the need for the hottest oven possible. The recipe was also erroneous in instructing the cook to bake the pudding for an hour before placing it under the meat. Yorkshire folk blame her error on her southern origins.

The Yorkshire pudding survived the wars of the 20th century as well as the food rationing of the '40s and '50s and sailed through the swinging '60s. As the pace of modern life picked up and more women worked outside of the home, cooking in the home started to decline. The rise of convenience foods and ready-made meals toward the end of the last century saw the invention of the first commercially produced Yorkshire puddings with the launch of the Yorkshire-based Aunt Bessie's brand in 1995.

In 2007, Vale of York MP Anne McIntosh campaigned for Yorkshire pudding to be given the same protected status as French champagne or Greek feta cheese. "The people of Yorkshire are rightly and fiercely proud of the Yorkshire pudding," she said. "It is something which has been cherished and perfected for centuries in Yorkshire."

At the time, Yorkshire pudding was deemed too generic a term, but that hasn't stopped Aunt Bessie's and two other pudding manufacturers from making another attempt for the protected status. Understandably, this has caused concern for everyone outside of Yorkshire who makes the puddings commercially, since they might have to rename their products Yorkshire-style puddings.

Today, the Yorkshire pudding is as popular as ever, whether home cooked, eaten at the thousands of restaurants across the UK serving a traditional Sunday lunch, or bought at the supermarket. On any given Sunday, expatriates and Brits throughout Europe tuck into Yorkshire pudding, and in Australia, New Zealand, and Canada puddings are still a large part of the food culture. Just why this simple mixture of flour, eggs, milk, and salt gained a place in the culinary heart of a nation and developed a worldwide reputation is a mystery which many have tried to solve, but have yet to answer. Maybe it is simply because Yorkshire puddings taste very good.

INGREDIENTS:

Makes 8 large Yorkshire puddings

3 large eggs

125g plain flour (4 ½ Oz)

½ tsp sea salt

150ml whole milk (half a cup)

Vegetable oil

COOKING INSTRUCTIONS:

Beat the eggs together in a mixing bowl using a balloon whisk.

Sift the flour with the salt, then gradually beat this into the eggs to make a smooth batter.

Whisk in the milk until combined. Cover and leave to stand at room temperature for about 1 hour.

Preheat the oven to 220°C/200°C fan/Gas 7.

Put 2 teaspoons of vegetable oil into each compartment of two 4-hole Yorkshire pudding tins (see tip, below). If you only have one tin, you'll have to do this and cook the Yorkshires in two batches.

Place the tin in the oven for 12-15 minutes to heat up the oil and tins until very hot (this is important for the rise).

Stir the batter and pour into a jug. At the oven (this is safer than carrying a tin of hot oil across the kitchen), carefully pour some batter into the middle of the oil in each hole, remembering that it is very hot. Watch out as the oil will sizzle a bit as the batter hits it.

Put the tins straight back into the oven and bake for about 15 minutes or until the Yorkshires are well risen, golden brown and crisp. Serve immediately with your choice of roast and all the trimmings.

What's next for Rex and Albert?

Cumberland Sausage Shocker

Baking. It can get a guy killed.

Following his nose, Albert is on the trail of a master criminal he chooses to dub 'The Gastro Thief'. In Cumbria, in the small town of Keswick, he begins to investigate but finds the trail cold.

It looks like a dead end, but when Rex digs up a body, everything changes fast.

Don't miss the next exciting instalment of their British culinary tour.

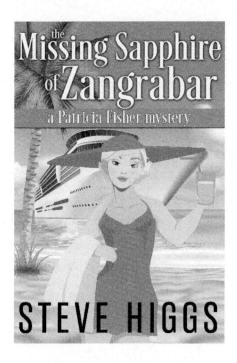

Read the book that started it all.

A thirty-year-old priceless jewel theft and a man who really has been stabbed in the back. Can a 52-year-old, slightly plump housewife unravel the mystery in time to save herself from jail?

When housewife, Patricia, catches her husband in bed with her best friend, her reaction isn't to rant and yell. Instead, she calmly empties the bank accounts and boards the first cruise ship she sees in nearby Southampton.

There she meets the unfairly handsome captain and her appointed butler for the trip – that's what you get when the only room available is a royal suite! But with most of the money gone and sleeping off a gin-fuelled pity party for one, she wakes to find herself accused of murder; she was seen leaving the bar with the victim and her purse is in his cabin.

Certain that all she did last night was fall into bed, a race against time begins as she tries to work out what happened and clear her name. But the Deputy Captain, the man responsible for safety and security onboard, has confined her to her cabin and has no interest in her version of events. Worse yet, as she begins to dig into the dead man's past, she uncovers a secret - there's a giant stolen sapphire somewhere and people are prepared to kill to get their hands on it.

With only a Jamaican butler faking an English accent and a pretty gym instructor to help, she must piece together the clues and do it fast. Or when she gets off the ship in St Kitts, she'll be in cuffs!

Tempest Michaels is about to have a bad week.

When a newspaper ad typo sends all manner of daft paranormal enquiries his way, P.I. Tempest Michaels has no sense of the trouble and danger heading his way.

In no time at all, he has multiple cases to investigate, but it's all ridiculous nonsense like minor celebrity Richard Claythorn, who believes he is being stalked by a werewolf and a shopkeeper in a nearby village with an invisible thief.

Solving these cases might be fun if his demanding mother (Why are there no grandchildren, Tempest?) didn't insist on going with him, but the simple case of celebrity stalking might not be all it seems when he catches a man lurking behind the client's property just in time to see him step into the moonlight and begin to transform.

All he wanted was a nice easy job where he got to be his own boss and could take his trusty Dachshunds to work. How much trouble can a typo cause?

The paranormal? It's all nonsense, but proving it might get him killed.

More Books by Steve Higgs

Blue Moon Investigations

Paranormal Nonsense

The Phantom of Barker Mill

Amanda Harper Paranormal Detective

The Klowns of Kent

Dead Pirates of Cawsand

In the Doodoo With Voodoo

The Witches of East Malling

Crop Circles, Cows and Crazy Aliens

Whispers in the Rigging

Bloodlust Blonde – a short story

Paws of the Yeti

Under a Blue Moon – A Paranormal Detective Origin Story

Night Work

Lord Hale's Monster

The Herne Bay Howlers

Undead Incorporated

Patricia Fisher Cruise Mysteries

The Missing Sapphire of Zangrabar

The Kidnapped Bride

The Director's Cut

The Couple in Cabin 2124

Doctor Death

Murder on the Dancefloor

Mission for the Maharaja

A Sleuth and her Dachshund in Athens

The Maltese Parrot

No Place Like Home

Patricia Fisher Mystery Adventures

What Sam Knew

Solstice Goat

Recipe for Murder

A Banshee and a Bookshop

Diamonds, Dinner Jackets, and Death

Frozen Vengeance

Mug Shot

The Godmother

Murder as an Artform

Wonderful Wedding and Deadly Divorces

Albert Smith Culinary Capers

Pork Pie Pandemonium

Bakewell Tart Bludgeoning

Stilton Slaughter

Bedfordshire Clanger Calamity

Death of a Yorkshire Pudding

Cumberland Sausage Shocker

Arbroath Smokie Slaying

Free Books and More

Get sneak peaks, exclusive giveaways, behind the scenes content, and more. Plus, you'll be notified of Fan Pricing events when they occur and get exclusive offers from other authors because all UF writers are automatically friends.

Not only that, but you'll receive an exclusive FREE story staring Otto and Zachary and two free stories from the author's Blue Moon Investigations series.

Yes, please! Sign me up for lots of FREE stuff and bargains!

Want to follow me and keep up with what I am doing?

Facebook

Printed in Great Britain
by Amazon

18418775R00139